Dishonorably Discharged 3

The Ex's Tour

By Desean Rambo

AF586062

All characters appearing in this work are fictitious.
Any resemblance to real persons, living or dead; is purely coincidental.

deseanrambo@boardgamemedia.com

CHAPTER 1

KATE

"Kate are you sure you are ok?" Tricia said to me as she stacked dishes in the kitchen. I looked like hell, felt like death, and probably welcomed its presence at that time. I was totally burnt out from work. My eyes were beyond bloodshot red. I was jet lagged.

I'd just arrived in the house from my eighth, maybe ninth, flight overseas. I don't know, I lost count by this time.

My career was doing well, really well, but my body and mind had suffered from my success. Oakleaf Furniture had fallen into a rapid international expansion and as usual they sent the only person fit for the job: *Kate Rowland.*

My ability to close accounts was becoming a bit of a burden. This company expected me to do everything except sweep the floors and turn off the lights at the end of the day. Don't get me wrong, I loved the money but I'd finally hit my breaking point.

Tricia snapped her fingers at me. "Wake up! Wake up! I'm talking to you," she hollered through the blurry haze that was my vision. I had no idea what she was talking about as she bobbed her head back and forth like a free range chicken. Everything in the last four months was a total blur in my mind.

First there was the dreaded ice storm which happened right on my birthday. Again I was soldiering up for Oakleaf when I nearly lost my life in an unexpected blizzard. Rashon and I went through a life threatening experience together in that blizzard that's changed our friendship forever. While we aren't dating, and possibly never will, we understand more than ever that we care about one another. That doesn't mean we haven't fooled around but no one has crossed the goal line, if you will.

"Kate?!" Tricia yelled again as my head bobbed in and out of consciousness. I finally came through and cleared out the cobwebs. I took a deep breath as I pulled from the depths of my soul to focus on every word she commanded to me.

"Kate do you hear me?!"

"Huh?"

"Kate, I said someone asked me about you the other day."

"Who, what, why?" I said in a growing haze.

Tricia put away the rest of the dishes and joined me at the wood dining table. "I said, this guy asked me about you. Tall white guy with long hair," she repeated.

"James," I said.

"Yeah, how do you know him?"

"He's *that guy.* Long story, but you remember most of it," I said.

"Oooh! He was talking about you in a really good way."

"I don't like the way you said that."

"What do you mean? He really likes you," Tricia said with a smirk that meant something rather than what she said.

"He really wants to bang me. I admire his consistency to his approach though. If you don't succeed at first then try again."

"Ok Aalyiah Rowland," Tricia teased. I hadn't seen her in weeks but it was just like I never left. That was my best friend, always doing her best to give me perspective.

She leaned over the table as she continued. "So when is the last time someone actually succeeded?"

My jetlag headache suddenly intensified. I wasn't up for a sermon today. I laid my head down like a tired fourth grader on the table and prepared to take a nap.

"Kate, you hear me talking to you."

"What?"

"So when's the last time someone has succeeded?" she repeated.

"I don't know," I said, "I don't want to talk about this right now."

"What happened in Europe?"

"Nothing, nothing happened in Europe," I repeated.

"Ok then. I am going to let you get some rest but we are going to talk about this later," she said.

Of course she already knew. I lied. A lot happened in Italy but it was too much to get into right then and there.

***

As I said earlier, Oakleaf somehow fell into a rapid global expansion. After I closed the Furniture Depot account things just blew up at work. My boss, Mr. Nixon, got a cold call from an Italian company that wanted to purchase a fleet of office furniture from us.

Now why would an Italian company want to do business with us and not a supplier in Italy? I was getting to that.

Our furniture was featured in several industry leading publications over the past year. Our competitive advantage is that we have furniture that can actually lower energy costs due to the material's heat absorption and cooling qualities. It's really nerdy science stuff, I am not even exactly sure how it works but I know how to sell it!

Since some of those publications are distributed worldwide it's only natural that we'd spark up interest overseas. But not like this. In the last four months things have gotten straight up crazy with the number of people wanting to see and feel the product up close. And that meant that Oakleaf had to send one person to close the sale. That person was the company MVP and the Senior Director of Sales, *Kate Rowland.*

The Italy account was the most nerve wrecking experience of my life. The first time I flew out everything seemed to be pretty cool. The first time I went out there I left on a Sunday to arrive Monday morning. In my carry-on I brought the samples of the desks so that they would have something they could see and touch while I gave the presentation.

It all was going to plan at first. Rashon happily dropped me off at the airport where I arrived just in time to go through the security and board in less than 20 total minutes. The flight was a eight hour flight into Rome. I had more than enough time to rest up, practice my pitch, and do some light meditation.

When I arrived in Rome that's when everything started going left. First of all there was no one waiting for me at the airport as we agreed. I waited over 2 hours before I had to pay $30 in American money for a taxi to take me approximately five miles to my hotel.

The hotel was ok but it was old and outdated. The bed was a twin sized rock hard bed that felt like it was made of rocks. The window was so tiny the room barely lit from the street lights outside. The shower was so small I could barely stand at a comfortable angle and actually get wet. And to top it off, there was no fridge. Again, this was another sign that my patience was going to be pushed to its limits.

The following day's meeting was uneventful. The whole thing was a complete waste of my time to say the least. I had no idea how

Italians traditionally negotiated but they seemed less than interested in buying anything.

I met with three guys, Gio, Andre, and Danny. Gio was the leader of the negotiators. The others said little as he and I talked about what Oakleaf had to offer them. I passed around my samples as I laid down my pitch, contract and pen in hand as usual.

“”

The three Italians giggled as they passed the sample around and listened to my pitch. They were a weird bunch to say the least. From what I knew, their company was a financial services company that basically sold unsuspecting Italians totally unnecessary loan insurance.

The leader of the bunch, Gio, finally stopped giggling long enough to ask me a question in return. He leaned back as his expression changed to a more serious tone.

“What will you have to drink?” he said, totally dismissing the sales pitch.

Being a total newbie to international customs I decided that while in Rome it was best to do as the Romans did.

“I’ll have whatever you have, respectfully,” I said as they cracked open a bottle and cranked out four wine glasses from thin air. This whole arrangement felt more like a dinner party than a serious business deal. In the back of my mind all I could think about was my commission payment of close to $25,000 if I could close them.

I took the moment to take it all in. The details were sketchy at best. The Italians dressed business casual in bright pink and teal button ups, unbuttoned to expose their chests and small gold chains. They drank alcohol in business meetings, they never once asked about numbers. *Were they serious? They sounded serious in the emails; they showed up, what was the hold up?*

"How is business in America?" Gio asked me with a big grin. His slick hair, teal shirt and gold chain gave me the vibe of the old wrestler Razor Ramon.

"Business is doing well. You know the American economy is all up-and-down, but we've carved out a nice little niche with the eco-friendly materials—"

"—is this your first time in Italy?" he cut me off. He was more interested in my travel experiences than spending money. I quietly exhaled my frustration and obliged the tangent.

"Yes, first time," I said with a bright fake smile.

Gio turned to his partners as they laughed in unison. There was an inside joke I wasn't getting.

"We have to take her out on the town! How rude!" Gio said with his hands outstretched. He hadn't taken a second look at the information I presented. *Whatever, I was in Italy and offered a free night of entertainment. What the hell, you live once.*

"Let's do it," I said.

That evening I joined the three businessmen at a dance club in Rome. It was unlike anything I'd ever seen. From wall to wall it was packed with people dancing and getting into the music. The electronic music played nonstop as neon lights shined in every direction. The crowd was really into it.

I was terribly overdressed in my work clothes but went with the flow anyways. As we arrived, Gio quickly got us set up with a round of shots before hitting the dance floor. This wasn't like an American club. Dancing wasn't an option; it was the *only* option.

I cannot lie. The club experience in Italy was among the funniest nights of my life. For what felt like four hours we danced, stomped, threw our hands up, and tossed back shots. I hadn't felt that alive in years. There was only one problem though… this still wasn't getting me any closer to getting a deal done.

At the end of the night Andre and Danny grabbed a cab, while Gio and I flagged down a separate cab. I wasn't going back to his place, but he didn't know that yet.

"So, where to young lady?" he asked with a grin.

"I have an early flight to catch in the morning," I replied. This was actually true. I had to be up at a crazy early hour.

"Back to America?" he asked as the cab jumped over the tiny potholes.

"Yes. Sadly."

"Why so soon?"

"I was only here for business," I said disappointingly.

"Maybe we can finish our business later?" he said with a larger smile.

"Of course," I replied.

A few minutes later we arrived at his place. He lived in a beautiful historic building with brick archways above the doors. I was breathtaking to see the way the light accented the brick and classic wood shutters.

"Take the lady where ever she needs," Gio instructed to the driver as he handed him a wad of cash. He looked back at me and smiled. I waved as he disappeared into the building. I knew this would not be my last time in Rome.

CHAPTER 2

By the time I came back home I was drenched with sweat from the stress. I had to break it to my bosses Mrs. Brenda and Mr. Nixon that I didn't close the sale with the Italians.

I had my script down pat just in the time the plane landed. I would simply tell my superiors that the Italians had a different negotiation style and didn't do business the same speed Americans do.

The next day, it was time to face the music.

"That should have been a slam dunk account," Mrs. Brenda said as we sat in her office together. She tapped the side of her glasses on her neatly organized wood desk. Her face had a look that asked if I really got any work done.

"The Italians negotiate completely different, they're hard to read," I said as I tried to guess her thoughts. "They want the product but they wouldn't engage in numbers talk. I swear I tried everything."

Mrs. Brenda sighed as she spun 180 degrees in her chain. Her blonde-white hair shined from a ray of sunlight as she checked over emails in her computer. "They haven't emailed us back yet. Let's play it by ear," she said.

I sighed as I slunk in my chair. I felt like a failure for the first time in a long time. I really wanted to be the triumphant company hero.

"How was Italy?" Brenda asked as she turned back towards me.

"It was good. I liked it," I said.

"That was your first time outside the country, right?"

"Second. My sister got married in Jamaica," I replied.

"So that was your first time in Europe?" she smiled.

“Yes.”

“I know they were on you Kate,” she said as she shook her head knowingly.

“What do you mean? I asked.

“There are two things European men love: African and American women,” she said.

“Oh… it wasn’t like that! I went over the pitch to a tee. They just didn’t receive it the way I expected,” I confessed.

“I don’t think you know what I mean. European men like to show off, impress women, then they’ll come down to earth once their validated,” she informed.

“Oh.”

“They’ll call back. And when you go back, you need to remember that.”

“I got it. Stroke the man’s ego,” I laughed.

“You got it.”

The rest of that day was another normal day at the office. I went through the motions semi-jetlagged. I can’t really remember anything else from that time; it just the beginning of the loop life was throwing me for.

***

Approximately two weeks after the first negotiations, I found myself waiting on another flight to Rome. Again, Rashon was my taxi to the airport. Our friendship was still growing, but we weren’t headed for that boyfriend-girlfriend area just yet. We still hadn’t gone beyond deep touching and kissing. Anyways, he sat with me in the terminal as we waited for my flight to take off.

“Look at you, Miss Globetrotter!” Rashon said as we sat shoulder to shoulder in the hard round terminal seating. His trademark cologne smelled like an amazing blend of cedar leaves as he rocked a scarf and wool jacket.

“I’m doing my best. Just trying to get up there with you entrepreneurs of the world,” I teased.

“Don’t try. Its way too much stress for way too little money,” he laughed. Though he never complained about money I knew he had some financial difficulties he would never share with Tricia or me.

“You got it,” I said as I rubbed his knee. It was five in the morning. There was hardly anyone in the airport at the time. I glanced over a few rows to an older couple sitting together so gently. The African gentlemen draped his arm over what looked to be his wife as she slept quietly. I’d guess they were about 50 years old. He flashed a bright toothy smile as we made eye contact.

“You two are so beautiful together,” he said to me with an obvious Nigerian accent.

Rashon glanced at him, and then glanced at me. It was his way of saying *what are we today?*

“Thank you,” I said as I smiled back.

“How long have you been together?” he asked.

Great. I thought to myself as Rashon leaned back for the show. He was anticipating the answer as well. In his mind this nonsense conversation held tremendous value to the course of our relationship.

I froze up. It was the first time I was forced to deal with this question by a stranger. I had no answer. I didn't want to say anything to offend Rashon, but at the same time didn't want to accidentally start a relationship right before I left the country. I said the only thing that made sense.

"It's complicated."

The man laughed. His hearty laugh filled the lonely terminal with a sense of love. He rubbed his wife's shoulders as he replied back.

"It's always complicated. That is why you have to trust the Lord to guide you my friend," he said.

Rashon nodded as he welcomed the advice. I forced a smile to get it over with.

"They say anything that is worth having is worth fighting for," the man said as he went back to minding his business. I breathed a breath of fresh air under my breath as the conversation ended. *Disaster avoided.*

"Kate we need to talk about something," Rashon said with a serious tone. My heart dropped. I was barely coherent. Again, it was way too early for this.

"I'm pregnant," he said, deadpanning the joke.

"You're stupid. That's what you are," I laughed.

Nine hours later I was back in Rome. This time was a little less rough than last time. I was mentally prepared for the grand theft auto style cab drivers, narrow streets, and small outdated hotel rooms. I checked in the same hotel I stayed in previously, went over my script and prepared to negotiate like a European. *When in Rome, do as the Romans.*

Brenda's advice played through my head on loop as we met at their offices again. This time I took the initiative to study the details of the office. The shady insurance officers seemed like they were making a lot of cash. Photos of the partners with random luxury vehicles, yachts, and European celebrities lined every wall in sight. There was even a framed signed Soccer jersey on one of the walls.

This time Gio and I met alone to hammer out the details.

"Good to see you again!" he said with a laid back tone that hopefully was good for business.

"What you didn't think I was coming back?"

"I thought you couldn't hang with us," he said cheerfully.

I laughed as I prepared to go into my pitch. Before I could get my folder open Gio stopped me. He was keen on avoiding the heavy negotiations.

"Have you ever been to the Coliseum?" he asked as if he suddenly remembered something important.

"No I haven't," I said.

He hopped up from his desk and threw his sunglasses on. "We must go right now. You have to see it. It's a once in a lifetime experience!"

From the looks of it there wasn't much heavy lifting going on in the office. There were a handful of employees manning the phones. The telemarketers were each in his or her world of canned scripts and lead driving. It actually reminded me of our outfit back stateside.

"I'll be back!" Gio yelled out at his army of cronies as he led me outside. His car was parked along the narrow street on the side of the building. It was one of the most beautiful vehicles I'd ever laid eyes on. The yellow Lamborghini Aventador was something I'd only seen on television. The car screamed luxury with its sleek angles, racing style tires and butterfly doors.

The car started up with the roar of a lion. The beautiful contraption was as powerful as its aesthetics. We ripped through the streets of Rome with no cares for about ten minutes. Then I saw it. The Coliseum.

It was one of the most awe-inspiring experiences I'd ever seen. I was staring at a scene I'd seen in history books for years. The half crumbled stone arena had the presence of giants. Instantly I felt the memories of the legendary, barbaric contests that encountered the very structure I was now a mere fifty feet away from.

Gio smirked as he circled around to find a place to park. I was in a total daze as we got out and approached the pantheon.

"What do you think? Amazing huh?" he asked.

"It's so gorgeous, so grand. You must be used to seeing it so often but I couldn't even imagine this in my wildest dreams."

"You never get used to it. This is where the gladiators played. I like to come here to get my inspiration, you know?" he asked in his broken accent. Everything about him said cut throat gangster businessman, from the slicked back jet black hair on his head, to the half-buttoned dress shirt, to the tailored pants and expensive loafers on his feet.

I took a moment to take it all in. The tourists whisked around me as I stood in awe at the tall stone structure. In the back of my mind we needed to talk about the business that brought me back to Rome but for now I was in full experience mode.

We toured the inside of the building with a group of tourists as I worked on making common conversation.

"So, how is business going if you don't mind me asking? You seemed like you're doing pretty well," I started as we trotted along the tour.

"I cannot tell you that. We are going public," he said with an air of arrogance. I dropped the thread in silence.

"Just kidding. Silly American rules. Even if we were public, why couldn't I talk about it? I never understood that about American business," he continued.

"Understood what?"

"Why do you guys try to make it so fair?" he cut through his thick accent.

"I don't know. That's the SEC. Our company is private so I don't have to worry about those things."

"I just don't get your country. It's *not* fair. You got rich people, poor people, and a few people in between, you know? But America plays as if you are all equal," he continued.

"You're right. I can't argue that. But how is business doing in Italy," I asked again.

"It's going great!" he said with the enthusiasm of a child in a candy store. "The more your country pretends and everyone struggles, the more money I make."

"How so?"

"When your stock market crashes, so does the European market, so does the Chinese market, so does the Japanese market, and so does the Brazilian market," he continued with a growing confident tone. I looked along the steps of the Coliseum as I envisioned the ancient Roman spectators who once sat there.

“So when everyone’s all scared because the markets are crashing, they need money. They look for loans. And naturally they don’t want to lose the money that’s saving their ass, so they insure it. And that’s when they give me money.” he went on. The sunlight was near blinding as it reflected off his chrome sunglasses.

“That’s one of the most impressive business models I’ve heard. I wonder why Americans don’t think like that,” I replied. He nodded as he took in the blatant compliment. “Do you think we can get this contract done sometime today?”

He paused as he outstretched his arms. It was a display of power. Here we were in the ancient Roman Coliseum in the midst of a modern day gladiator fight, except this one was held in passive aggressive negotiations and on paper.

“I’m trying to show you who we are,” he boasted. “We aren’t supposed to sit behind desks and squabble about numbers. That’s not how our forefathers built civilizations. *This is how. This is life.*”

“With all due respect,” I said, “I appreciate everything but I came out here on good faith that we’d get a deal done.”

“*Faith.* You said it yourself. Keep the faith. Now what will be having for dinner?”

It was a question that had more than one answer. I knew in the pit of my stomach if I decline the dinner request there would be no deal done. The last thing I needed was to return to the states with no contract. I couldn’t make any more excuses to my bosses at this point. I was stuck. Dinner wouldn’t hurt anyone.

“I’ll go to dinner with you, sure. Whatever is good,” I obliged.

“That sounds perfect.”

CHAPTER 3

My first dinner in Rome was an unexpectedly fun experience. Gio was the consummate host, no matter how slimy his business tactics were. We dined at a quaint formal restaurant with large detailed murals on the walls and subtle ambient lighting. It was more of a spot for lovers, not business people in the midst of a five to six figure negotiation.

"I'll have a bottle of Montrachet, the chicken linguini, and whatever the lady will be having," Gio boasted. We'd arrived immediately from the Coliseum. It was still kind of early in the day for dinner by my standards but I was in no place to complain.

"I'll have the chicken as well," I said to the waiter. He resembled a matador with his formal outfit. It was unlike any American restaurant uniforms I remember.

"You'll like this place; it's the best food for 50 kilometers," he bragged. I looked on silently. "*Kilometers*. My fault, 30 miles."

I laughed as he corrected himself for my sake.

"You Americans and your metric system. Everything has to be unique in America. I don't get it," he commented.

"That's how it is. We don't question it. They tell us pounds and miles, so that's what we use," I replied.

"That's the problem. Your country breeds people who don't think," he boasted. I found myself slightly offended.

"How so?"

"This is a good example. I can tell by your face that you are upset we aren't sitting around pounding a negotiating table and counting numbers," he revealed. He was slightly right, but I wouldn't let him know that.

"I am here for business but I have no problem enjoying my company," I retorted.

"But you have a set idea how this should go," he clarified.

Before I could respond our dining arrived. I quickly got to the food as I tried to clear my mind and enjoy the experience. I'd never had the opportunity to experience another culture so intimately so I appreciated the moment however brief.

The food was amazingly good. The chicken was fresh, juicy, and flavored just right with lemons and spices. I never had a reason to doubt the cuisine but it was definitely better than expected.

"Kate, how long have you been with Oakleaf?" Gio asked me. He wiped his hands as he finished up his meal.

"A few months. Less than a year," I answered. "Why? What's up?"

"I was just wondering. Do you like sales? The traditional American way, I mean," he continued.

"It's ok. It pays the bills," I said back.

"You should think about coming to Europe. You'd make so much money. I see many Euros in your future," he contemplated. The inflection in his voice was as if he was cooking up a scheme.

"Many Euros, huh? What are you thinking?"

"Euros are the place to be. The American dollar is too volatile but that's beyond the point. Check this out, what do you think about valets?"

“Giovanni, are you asking me if I want to be a prostitute? That’s absolutely not going to happen!” I screamed in a low stern voice.

“No, no, no! You have it all backwards. Valets are pretty companions. Arm candy,” he said quickly in his accented voice. “There are rich guys all over the world that would pay for a pretty girl like you to accompany them to events.”

This is what Mrs. Brenda warned me about. She was right. They had a thing for black women. I was flattered but I wasn’t going to entertain the offer for more than one second.

“I appreciate the offer but no thank you. That’s not what I’m here for,” I said firmly.

“Ok, ok. If you say so, let’s get on then,” he replied. He flagged down the waiter and paid the tab as we continued to leave. “If you’ll follow me to my place we’ll talk about that contract.”

Finally. I’d put up with way too many diversions to leave now. It was time to get what we both came here for. It was time to seal the deal and finally get this thing over with.

Or so I thought.

***

“This is the place I call home for now,” Gio said as we entered his condo. The spacious top floor home was just as impressive inside as the external brick structure on the outside. True to European chic there were high walls and stone walls.

“Make yourself comfortable,” he hollered as he took his shoes off and disappeared to one of the back rooms. I could hear a door open and something rattled about as I sat in the posh living room. The couch was a dark suede with a matching ottoman right in front a set of large arched windows that displayed Rome perfectly.

He finally emerged holding two wine glasses, a vintage bottle, and decked in what looked like Gucci house shoes. I took one of the glasses as he sat next to me.

“1982, you have to try this,” he urged.

“I feel like I’m being seduced,” I muttered as I drank the spicy, sweet wine.

“So, let me see this contract,” he said as he put back his glass. I handed him my folder with the proposed contract inside. Finally, he cracked open the contract and gave it a glance. Within seconds he put it back in my hands.

“Done. That’s easy enough,” he said. I held back the relief I felt going through my body. No matter what he said the deal was not done until he wired the funds. But for now I could relax just a little knowing he finally actually read the deal.

“Let’s put a seal on the deal,” he said with a mysterious tone. His eyebrows arched with a devilish expression.

“What do you have in mind?” I asked.

“Let me show you,” he said as he rose from the seat.

I felt my heart palpitate as he drew closer and closer. His breath tickled my neck as he nibbled the nape and worked down. I let out a deep gasp and let myself go.

The fingers worked their ways down my sides. I closed my eyes and enjoyed the tingling sensations from each of his flowing fingertips. My body ached for the contact; this was a moment to remember.

My breath shortened. The moment grew, the perspiration intensified. His fingers made their way to their mark, sliding my silk underwear to the side. There was no resistance to the advance as the fingers did work. I moaned slowly and softly as the motion intensified. The walls pulsated as I went away into a place of ecstasy.

***

Every muscle in my arms burned as I dragged my luggage trough the airport terminal. After a stressful, confusing, business deal I was finally back on American soil. I was home.

“She’s back!” Rashon yelled from across the airport. He ran to help me as I struggled to make progress with my bags.

“What’s up?” I asked as he unloaded the bags from my failing biceps.

“You look so stressed. What happened?” he asked as we walked through the terminal.

“Nothing. Just a lot of work,” I replied.

“So, did you get the deal done or whatever?”

“Of course I got the deal. That’s what I do,” I boasted.

“Then it was worth it. You can sleep when you’re dead,” he joked.

“If only you knew the half of it,” I began, “I just can’t wait to get back in my own bed.”

“I feel you,” he said as we got outside. He loaded the bags into his tiny Mazda “Bentley” and we took off.

“The dog tags. You’re finally wearing them,” he noticed as he steered along the freeway.

“Oh. Yeah. I decided to bring them with me. You got a problem with that?” I teased.

"They're yours. Wear them whenever you want. I don't care," he dismissed. "Anyways, how was Greece?"

"Rome, that's in Italy," I corrected.

"Rome, Greece, same thing," he retorted.

"It's not the same. Anyways, it was cool. I got to do a little sightseeing. We went to the Coliseum, and some restaurants and stuff," I said.

"Oh. *We?"* he said with a knowing tone.

"The client. You know how it is. You have to build a relationship with the client before they buy," I proposed.

"Sounds like it was fun. I'd like to see the world one day. I just can't afford to travel like that. One day I will though," he reminisced as we approached Tricia's neighborhood quickly.

"Maybe we can go on a trip one day," I offered. The expression on his face didn't change. I could tell he didn't take the consideration serious. He simply grunted at the idea as he pulled the car to a park in front of the house. We were here.

"So you remember where you live?" Tricia yelled as I stumbled in a daze.

"Yes. I'm here!" I said as I outstretched my arms like Mary Poppins. Tricia was dressed up in some new designer couture. Business must be doing well at the boutique. The number of clothes in her home inventory was significantly reduced.

"How is work doing?" I asked as I walked down our newly clean hallway. I almost didn't recognize it without the miscellaneous bags and shoe boxes.

"Girl I can't keep anything in. I've been working."

Finally I was in my room. I hopped onto my bed like a puppy in a doggie bed. The familiar warmth of my comforter took me away as my body slowly shut down to recuperate from the day of traveling.

Knock. Knock. I totally forgot Rashon was behind me. He threw my luggage on the floor as I sank deeper into my nap.

"You good?" he asked as he sat on the edge of my bed. His brown boots matched his black t shirt and dark blue jeans. I could tell his vibe was off. I wondered what it was.

"I'm just a little jetlagged, what's good with you? What have you been up to since I've left?"

"Nothing. Same old, same old," he began, then checked his cell, "You might want to know I went on a couple of blind dates."

It hit my stomach like a thousand bricks. I felt a tightening pressure in my chest. I did my best to play it off.

"What? You dating? Who? When did you start dating? I have to see this to believe it," I chuckled.

"POF dates. Plenty of Fish. It's a dating website. I made a profile up there to see what happens," he responded.

"And what happened?"

"I went on two dates so far. The first with this older Russian chick. The photos were misleading. She did not look like the pictures at all. Not in a bad way but she had clearly aged since the photos were taken. She was nice, not too crazy, but we really had nothing in common. So I never hit her back."

"Did you smash?" I asked.

"Of course not. I probably could have if I wanted, honestly. Those older women don't have all of the hang-ups you young girls have."

"Oh please. Anyways, second date. Continue the story," I demanded.

"The second chick was cool. She's actually really nice. She kind of reminds me of you a tiny bit. She's from St. Kitts or something like that, you know, Caribbean like you. There was a little language barrier so she touched me a lot to demonstrate things. I think that really opened things up. She seems cool. I'm probably going to see her up again and see where it goes."

"I'm not sure about you and this internet thing. Can't you just meet people the regular way?" I said with a growing concern.

"When I try that, I end up being *friends* with the girl. *Isn't that how I got here?*"

"Just because we are friends today, that doesn't mean things can't change in the future. Just let things happen on their own," I assured.

"Yeah, yeah, yeah. I've heard this before. Let your actions say something for once. Time waits for no man," he said firmly. With that he got up and turned the lights of so I could finish my nap.

"Rashon," I hollered to him, "thanks again for picking me up. And good luck with the girl. I want you to be happy."

"No problem."

The Rome deal opened up doors we never knew existed. Over the next few weeks I flew to France, Wales, and England as I closed deal after deal in our global expansion. The English countries were much more American in their ways and I was able to negotiate normally using harsh deadlines and reverse circumstances.

Over the four week course I closed close to a half million dollars worth of sales. I singlehandedly created a global expansion that was set to more than double the value of the company. It goes without saying I was rewarded handsomely for my efforts. I was set to bank in over $100,000 in commissions alone on top of my salary. I'd become financially successful beyond my wildest dreams, but my love life was still a mess.

CHAPTER 4

RASHON

Kate wasn't happy to hear about my POF dates, but what was I supposed to do? I couldn't wait on her forever. I'm going to be 30 soon and that clock is ticking. Women have a biological clock but men have what I call a societal clock. In your teens and early twenties it's the cool thing to be the solo dolo single guy. The player, if you will.

But sometime around 28 it becomes weird. Your parents start hinting you need to bring someone home. Your aunts start trying to set you up on dates. Your friends slowly drop the "pimp" and "playa" narratives because they know the truth. You aren't single by choice. You're lonely, and if there was something you could do about it you would.

That's the place I was in life. It's a weird place to be in and one of the most exhausting things I've ever endured. On a daily basis I was bombarded with all these feelings I had no idea what to do with, and my friendship with Kate wasn't helping figure things out. If I was going to get past this phase it would come from decisions from within. Something inside me wanted to have someone there for me and if it wasn't going to be Kate, or Kimberly, then I would have to meet new people.

The first date was ok. It was with this woman named Alice. She was an older white lady, from Russia. Her photos showed a thin blonde girl with high cheekbones and long legs. The person I actually met was about five years older than the girl in the photos.

I couldn't get a read on if she liked me or just was looking for someone to blow her back out. I got the feeling it was the latter. She wasn't interested in continuing any threads of conversation. She was more biding time until I asked her to come back to my place. I wasn't interested in anything that easy off the jump so I kept it cordial and quickly deleted her number once I got home.

The second date was the one with potential. I paid the upgraded fee for the site so I had access to extra features. One of those features was that I could see who viewed my profile. This pretty 21 year old caramel-brown skin girl named, Mari. She was from St. Kitts or somewhere like that. She was above and beyond the finest girl to check my profile.

I went for broke and sent her a message. Her profile was sparse so I sent a vanilla message that simply read:

> *"What's up? I read your profile and thought you were pretty cool. Hit me up."*

That simple message always got the job done. Within a day she responded and we set the date up. We did a ice cream date at Coldstone Creamery. I didn't want to spend a bunch of money and have the option to leave at any given moment if her photos didn't match. Coldstone's outdoor tables were perfect for my plan.

When she arrived I was floored. She looked even *better* than the photos! She reminded me of a mix between the singer Ashanti and the actress Lauren London. She was five foot two and thick in all the right places. Suddenly, I felt my heart forgetting about my hopes with Kate.

Mari rocked slim jeans that accentuated her best features along with a regular t shirt and jacket. Her style was that of a 21 year old girl fresh out of college, youthful but still sexy.

"Hello," she said in a broken accent that pronounced the word hollow. I didn't even care. She was fine and I wasn't about to mess this up.

I got our ice creams and led her to the outdoors table. Even though she was fine I still had to reserve my option to dash to my car if anything crazy happened.

"So what do you do?" I asked.

"I am nurse assistant," she said. Her English wasn't very good.

"Where are you from again," I asked.

"St. Kitts."

"Oh ok. I asked because I like your accent," I replied. She blushed at the compliment.

She in return asked what I did for a living and I told her a little about the limousine business. Truth be told, business wasn't going well. I was up to my eyeballs in past due bills with little to no clients coming in. I had a nest egg big enough to survive for a few months so I wasn't at the wall yet but I was close.

All my energy up to that point had gone into my business and trying to cultivate my friendship with Kate and Tricia. I always felt if I had that unconditional support I could get to the next level.

"How long have you been in the states?" I asked.

"Six years," she replied as she continued blushing. If I didn't know any better I'd say she was smitten. I played it cool and made regular conversation to see where her head was at.

Our conversation went really well. I was intrigued by her sense of youth, helpfulness and positive energy. The only small problem was the language barrier as her native language was some form of broken English which I had a hard time following. All in all the date was a success.

***

"So I hear you're dating now," Tricia proclaimed as we grabbed lunch.

We hit a local soul food spot that served really good homemade food. With my light schedule and Tricia's night heavy workload at the boutique, we were finding time to get together for lunch on a near daily basis.

"Something like that," I said as I picked out the combo I wanted.

"Something like what? Are you taking this girl serious or not?" Tricia asked with the tone of a detective on the *First 48*. At this point I was sure anything I said would get back to Kate.

"It's only been one date. You can calm down. Stop trying to press me for information," I retorted.

"You have to know if you like her or not."

"She's cool. Hopefully we go on a second date and play it from there," I said.

"Ok," she mumbled as she perused the menu.

"I'm not going to sit around and pretend I don't want to get to know her on that level. I'm just not in the mood to have my time wasted by anymore females. Real talk, I'm about to give up," I said.

"You're smart, handsome, and funny. You can't give up," Tricia reassured me.

"Yes the hell I can. Being a good guy isn't worth it anymore in this society. Women want to spend their whole youth having fun and giving it all away to the fun guys then switch up when *they* want to. I'm not supposed to have a memory of this? I'm telling you Tricia, these women have me so jaded."

"So why even date now if you feel that way?" she asked.

"It's my last chance to get a young girl before she gets totally whored out in her twenties. If it doesn't happen now it's not going to happen. I can't be in my mid thirties still trying to holler at 21 year olds. It just wouldn't look right.

"That's where society has it all wrong. Like, I'm supposed to build myself up and be responsible my whole twenties while my future wife clubs every night and does whoever. Then when we hit our thirties I'm supposed to act like I didn't get dissed by these women, pick one, and live happily ever after? Nah, hell nah," I finished.

"You're right. But you got issues brother," she laughed.

"I feel like we have this conversation all the time. Am I wrong?!"

"Yes in a way, but every woman is not the same. Look at me for instance. I don't date. I don't go to the clubs. I just do my thing and if someone comes by then so be it."

"Yeah but that's rare. Most cats are intimidated by you so the ones that step to you are the alpha males. A man has to have his stuff together to step to you. *You fancy. Hair done, nails done, everything did,*" I joked.

"Whatever, whatever," Tricia said as she changed the subject. "How is work going?"

"It's slow man," I said, "you know how it is."

"I'm worried about you sometimes," she said as she picked out her food.

"I'm fine Tricia. You ain't got to worry about me. I'm going to be alright. Believe that."

CHAPTER 5

KATE

"Watch me pick up this spare though!" I yelled back at Rashon and Tricia as I tiptoed down the slippery polished lane.

It was the first time in a long time we all had time to meet up together so we decided to spend the evening bowling. None of us were any good at it, nor did the fact that Tricia and I were drinking like we were trying to get drunk help as well.

DING! POW! The pins clashed alongside the force of the ten pound ball. I picked up the spare. I did my best touchdown dance as I teased them.

"Please never dance again. You dance like a dead duck falling out of the sky," Rashon joked.

Tricia and I were too gone by then, the rest of the game we danced whether we hit one pin or no pins at all. It was a fun time. I hadn't been out with my crew in a long time. It didn't even matter who won the game as long as we laughed and had a good time.

Before we could even finish the game Rashon started acting weird. I noticed he was constantly checking his phone and smirking as he punched his thumbs into the screen. This was a new behavior for the quiet one.

"Are you going to bowl or are you going to play on your phone?" I said as I looked at him with a drunken frown.

"Oh, my bad," he said as he robotically stood, grabbed his ball, rolled it, and returned to his phone. I was beginning to get annoyed with whatever he was giving his attention to. He was killing my vibe.

“Rashon,” I said with growing agitation, “are you going to talk to us or the phone? We came here to spend time together. Whatever you are doing can wait, put your phone up.”

“Nah this can’t wait,” he said as he looked on. Tricia and I were both now leaning over our seats barely sober to make heads or tails of the game. I think I was winning.

“It was fun hanging out but I have to get you two home, then I have to catch up with a buddy,” he said in a panic. He rushed to get our coats and shoes like a school chaperone on a field trip.

“Let’s go ladies!”

“But we aren’t even done with the game,” I said. He slapped the reset button.

“We’re done now.”

Minutes later Tricia and I were returned home safely. Rashon hurried us inside then sped off to go take care of more pressing matters. I was irritated by his whole demeanor.

Inside, Tricia and I grabbed some water and leftovers as we sobered up. She wasn’t too affected by Rashon’s actions. Maybe she knew something I didn’t.

“That doesn’t bother you?” I asked as I sat down at the dining table.

“What?” Tricia responded as the microwave beeped to zero and she retrieved the steaming plate of food. We picked over it with two forks.

“The way he’s acting, that was weird,” I said.

“Oh that? That’s nothing,” she assured.

“So you know what that is all about? Do tell.”

“I don’t know much but I do know he is starting to date now.”

"You aren't trying to date him. I don't see why it's a problem," Tricia said as she started to sober up. The conversation officially killed my buzz.

"That's not the point. How are we going to let him chase behind some girl he met online? That doesn't even make sense! He's smarter than that! Only people with something to hide date online," I snapped back.

"It sounds like someone is jealous Kaitlyn."

"I just don't want to see him get hurt. He deserves better than that," I added.

Tricia rolled her eyes. She wasn't buying it. "Then date him."

"Didn't we already try that? I care about him so much; I just don't feel that romantic flame. There's something definitely there though, I just wish I knew what it was," I said as I slunk my head on the table into my folded arms.

"You need to tell that boy how you feel then. Stop beating around the bush."

"You're not funny," I sneered. "If there was something romantic there I think it would have already happened."

"You're not giving it a chance. You haven't given anything a chance but your career these last few months," Tricia said truthfully.

"I don't have time to put in any guy..."

"I have a suggestion. Go on an ex's tour."

"An ex's tour?" I raised my head back up to make sure she wasn't drinking again. This sounded like the dumbest thing I ever heard but I let her finish.

"An ex's tour. You allot specific dates, the same amount of time, to all of the men in play. Put it all on the table so there is no more confusion. After the tour is over you'll have a clear understanding of what you want and don't want. You might even end up with someone you'd least expect."

"I don't like this idea, it feels too contrived. This is almost too good to be true," I said as I lumbered out of my seat and headed to bed.

"Think about it. Put it this way, you can't move on if you're constantly looking in the rearview."

"I'll think about it. I'll see you in the morning."

***

RASHON

It was nice to hang out with my girls Kate and Tricia for once in a while, but it wasn't like old times. Usually I'd join in the festivities while we all embarrassed ourselves and have fun but no longer. I finally realized that if I was ever going to get what I desired in life I would have to start being a little more selfish, even if it hurt my friends.

As soon as Mari started texting me during the bowling session I knew I had to find a way to get out of there. The old me would have done my best to appease everyone but no longer. It only mattered what I wanted and right now. What was more important was seeing where this new thing was headed. I already knew where I stood with the ladies who were in my company.

"What are u doing?" Mari texted as I watched Kate and Tricia almost bust their asses while dancing on the polished lanes.

"Hanging out," I texted back. We still only had one date under our belts but we'd text sporadically on a daily basis.

"What are you getting into," I sent back as Kate hurled insults at me.

"I'm getting my hair done," she replied. *I didn't want to hear this. What did this have to do with me?* Then she texted the magic words…

"I want you to come see it."

Bingo! In my mind that was the green light I was looking for. That was the fail proof sign I never got from Kate. Why else would she get her hair done just for me to see it? She was trying to impress me. This girl was putting in work, and that work would be appreciated.

I quickly formulated a plan to get Kate and Tricia's drunk asses off the lanes and took them home. I literally pushed them out of the car and pulled them into their own home. I left them to continue their party at the kitchen table while I rushed to text Mari back.

"Where are you?" I texted as I pulled the car in drive and got out of Tricia's neighborhood.

"At my cousin's house," she sent back. *Great.* She had someone else with her. This was not what I had in mind. I took a break to pull into a BP station. I let the fumes from the gas slowly take my mind off the state of panic and fall into a brief euphoria.

DING! DING! I snapped out of it.

DING! DING! My phone clamored from the barrage of texts.

"I'm done now.

“Where are you?

“Are you coming?

“Do you need my address?”

Holy crap. This girl was blowing my phone up. She really wanted to see me. I wasn’t used to this kind of attention.

“Send me your address.” I sent back.

DING! DING! She immediately texted back her address for the GPS. I did a Tiger Woods fist pump as I finished pumping my gas and headed on over.

She stayed in a modest apartment community, upstairs on the third floor. The tension in my stomach grew each step of the hike up to her place. I wasn’t really nervous but the tension was tight. We hadn’t even been on a second date and I was visiting her home.

KNOCK! KNOCK! I took a deep breath as I tapped on her door lightly. She snatched the door open in an instant. I was floored. She was already a cute girl but tonight she looked amazing. Her curly black hair was all done up in some kind of ponytail. Her makeup was carefully done and she smelled really good. She was going all out to impress me.

“Come in!” she said.

I glanced around the place as I stepped in. It looked like your normal chick spot with dark furniture and matching granite countertops. The only odd thing was that this girl didn’t have any posters of iconic female celebrities like Audrey Hepburn and Marilyn Monroe all over her walls. Instead, she displayed what looked like old family photos from the islands. I was impressed.

“So, who lives with you?” I asked.

"No one. This is my place," she said. How a 21 year old afforded such a nice apartment I had to know.

"Nursing must do well," I said as we took a seat on the couch.

"I do alright. Enough to pay the bills and send money back home," her accented voice replied. She had on some dark blue leggings that showed off everything and a pink crop top to match. I don't think I ever had a girl this fine actually into me. I played it calm regardless.

"What's up with your cousin, where is she?"

"She's at her place," Mari said back with a devilish grin as she squeezed up next to me. "Do you like my hair?"

"I do. It looks really good. You did all this for me?"

"Maybe," she said as she rubbed my bicep. "What do you want to do?"

"I'm cool with whatever you want to do," I replied. There was a hint of apprehension in my voice. Maybe things were indeed going too fast. I barely knew this girl.

"You're so warm," she said as she began to rub my stomach area. I fell myself falling into her seduction. I was hopeless to an island girl's spell. I already knew this.

"No, no. Don't move. I just want to feel your warmth. I'm not going to do anything," she whispered in my ear. I was too far gone now.

The next thing I knew she was talking me into talking off my shirt as we laid there on the couch. Then she took off her shirt to feel the "body on body heat." Soon after, she was unbuckling my pants. She continued her spiel.

"I'm not going to do anything," she said as she kneeled down and removed my belt. My pants came off. *Suddenly wetness was all around me, but I'm no island.* I gave up resisting and closed my eyes as the moment carried me off planet earth and into euphoria. All my problems and frustrations were second thoughts as Mari worked her mouth like a hydraulic pump.

I stared off into space as she took me to another place. *What did I do to deserve this?* It didn't matter because it felt so good.

***

KATE

"You are not divorcing! You are going to Jamaica to speak with my pastor! You will go right now!" my mother screamed through the phone.

The funny thing is that for all of the times my mother threatened me, I'd never been to the island one time in my life. As a third generation I was so detached from my family still down there they might as well be distant ancestors. I had no concept of them beyond a photo or old wise tale. One of such wise tales involved the witch doctor pastor who had a soup for everything.

My mother wanted the best for me, but not over what she felt God wanted. As a second generation her mind was too far embedded with the old tales that they were genuinely real to her. I knew she was all bark and no bite so I let her scream at me until she lost her breath.

"Mom, mom!" I said, "It's done. It's been over for a while."

"And how long is a while huh?" she said between gasps.

"A year."

"Oh God no! Noooo! She doesn't know what she does," my mother prayed into the speaker.

"Mom! Mom! Listen to me. We tried like I told you we would. It didn't work. It is over."

She knew about the incident, but my mother was under the impression we reconciled and lived happily ever after. Unfortunately that was not the case. I helped calm my mother down and shortly hung up the phone. I took a big exhale. *Finally, that was over.*

KNOCK! KNOCK!

Tricia was already in so it could only be one person. I put my phone down as I heard Tricia open the door for him. He slid in the kitchen in his socks like Tom Cruise in risky business. Something good must have happened to him. He's never that animated.

"What's gotten into you?" I asked with an eyebrow raised.

"Nothing. Nothing," he said. "A brother can't be happy sometime?"

"Not that damn happy. Did you get some from this new girl?" I asked as I scrolled through my phone.

"I wish. I wish," he said. "But she's cool though, real cool."

"Oh, sounds cool. Listen, I did what you told me to do," I continued.

"What? I don't remember. Fill me in." He was now dancing like James Brown in front of me.

"I called my mother. I came clean," I slowly revealed. The dancing stopped.

"Wow Kate. That's big. I'm proud of you. How did she take it?"

"Not well of course. She threatened me, cursed me, and then she said she's going to call her pastor for me."

"The crazy one?" he asked.

"Yup. You already know. They are probably going to sacrifice a neck bone or some chicken blood or something else crazy," I loathed.

"Keep the faith," he teased. If looks could kill, I would have stared 100 bullets through his cranium. "I believe in that stuff," he divulged.

"Yeah but you're always following that hokey-pokey new age crap. I'm sorry, I believe in the real world where my ex husband chose marijuana over his wife and future!"

"You got to believe!" Rashon shrugged as he did a Jackson Five spin. I couldn't help but chuckle.

"We should do something," I said.

"We just did. You didn't have enough fun bowling?"

"I mean we as in just you and I."

"Are you asking me on a date Kaitlyn?" he asked with a inquisitive look. I almost died laughing as he held out the ends of his blazer like Michael Jackson, complete with neck movements.

"No. I'm asking if you want to do something. I don't want to blow your head up any bigger than it is right now."

"Are you scared of losing me? Is that why the sudden change of heart?" he said as he stopped dancing.

"I'm just making better decisions now. More informed decisions."

"About what? What does this have to do with me?"

"Everything."

CHAPTER 6

The ex's tour was officially starting. At least I thought so. I'd go out with each guy from my recent past in the hopes that one of them was *the one*, or I'd leave with a clear picture of exactly the type of mate I didn't want. Tricia was right. It'd been way too long. It was time to get back out there and face this dating this head on. Hell, even Rashon did!

That's another thing. I had to make a decision on him quickly as we both knew there was another contender. The poor guy waited long enough.

Things at work finally went back to normal. There weren't any more international clients blowing up our phones. The wave of positive PR across the pond seemed to have died down. My bosses didn't like that but I welcomed the end of the craziness. I was the one putting in those long hours, not them! I didn't even have the time or the energy to enjoy all the commissions I'd stacked up off Europe.

My young coworker Aryn was still going through her drama with her daughter's father. She was now coming to me for advice on a near daily basis. Taking care of her now three year old and balancing a relationship that was falling apart was having its toll on her. The once youthful thin blonde girl was losing her steam right before me.

I felt a responsibility to lead her through it.

We sat together in the break room after work while she struggled to hold tears back.

"Ms. Kate I don't know what to do anymore. I know he's with other girls but when I see him with my daughter… I can't take her from him. He makes her so happy. She needs her father," Aryn said as she slumped in a cold steel folding chair.

"I understand," I said. I didn't understand. I didn't have children of my own but the poor girl needed help. She couldn't tell which way was up. Many days she came into work with *that look* I knew too well.

"It's going to hurt your daughter more to be around the fighting. Eventually you're going to have to cross that road. I can't tell you what to do, but remember your decisions affect her too," I continued.

She nodded as she wiped her flowing eyeliner. The poor girl did not want to go home.

"I wish I could leave," she said, "I'd just run away and leave it all behind."

"I know, I know," I said as I rubbed her back. She was shaking uncontrollably. There was something else underneath her fear. Something bigger than cheating and arguing. Something I knew too well.

"Aryn can I ask you something? You don't have to answer if you don't want to."

"Yes."

"Has he hit you?"

She covered her face with both hands and bawled. The tears and shaking wouldn't stop. She didn't have to answer. I knew the answer.

"Oh my God. You could have told me. You can tell me anything," I said softly.

"I'm so scared Ms. Kate. He said he'd kill me if I left."

"I was there. My husband hurt me as well," I said. "Life goes on. You have to press on past this. You can do it. I did it."

She shook her head no as the sniffles continued.

“Yes. YES YOU CAN! There are people that will help you. There are things you can do. Is there somewhere you and your daughter can go?”

“No, my mother is in prison. And my father is just as bad. He drinks and does the same stuff,” she said painfully.

“You can end this. You have the power,” I preached from experience. “How much longer are you going to let this go on? Until you are dead and your daughter has no mother?”

She calmed the sniffling as she thought about it. Finally she came to an answer.

“I want out. Whatever it takes.”

“Where is your daughter? Can you get her now?”

“She’s at daycare. My friend watches her while I’m at work.” she replied.

“This is what I want you to do. I want you to get your daughter and go to a hotel. If you need anything call me. Don’t worry about work; I’ll take you off the schedule. Take all the time you need.”

“What about him? He’s going to be mad,” she said terrified.

“That’s why you call the police. It ends now. It ends tonight. Make the decision Aryn. This is not just your life that’s at stake. If he will put his hands on you, what is he going to do when your daughter gets older? Think about how you feel about your father. Sometimes the best love is from a distance.”

***

“So tonight’s the first?” Tricia said as I picked out an outfit for the evening. The ex’s tour was finally under way. I toyed with different combinations of tops and pants in the mirror as Tricia coached me from the side of my room.

“So what do you plan on doing?” she said.

“We’re just going to a bar and that’s it,” I replied.

“You liar. You’re going to put it on him, I know you,” Tricia teased. She knew I was going out with Rashon but wasn’t as surprised as I thought she would be.

“I’m just going to have a good time. Whatever happens is whatever happens. We can’t pretend like we aren’t regular people. If there is something there we’ll see. That’s the whole point of this thing, right?”

Tricia smiled as she picked out an outfit for me. She laid out a pair of skinny jeans with a white top and assorted costume jewels to top it off. It was casual, but still sexy. It worked good enough.

“Here is the thing, this is just a test,” I said. “I’m more interested in what he’s going to do. We’ve know each other all this time and he hasn’t made a solid move on me yet.”

Minutes later the doorbell rang. In walked Rashon with a poorly hidden smirk on his face. He was decked out in black jeans with a plain t shirt and gold chain. His style was noticeably changed from the usual button ups and blazers.

“What’s up?” he said as he looked me up and down. “Are you ready to do this?”

“As ready as you are,” I said.

“Whatever Kate. Let’s do this,” he said with a new swagger I didn’t recognize.

“What’s gotten into you? I feel like I’m talking to a different person right now.”

“You mad right now?” he joked as he answered my question with a question. I pushed him as we headed for the door. Tricia waved us out as we headed for his car.

“How’s everything going with work?” I said as he pulled out the driveway.

“I’m doing alright. Money comes, money goes. You know? I can’t stress about it anymore. As long as I got a roof over my head and some food I’ll make it another day,” he said.

“If you’re not doing well you know you I’ll help you out,” I offered.

“I’m fine. I don’t live with excuses, I can take care of myself,” he snapped.

“I’m sorry…”

“Kate, we are on a date. Stop making it weird. You’re the one making it weird now,” he retorted as he drove to the hotel bar we planned to hit up.

It was a quiet little corner of a bar, dimly lit with bar stools and sports playing on televisions. Rashon wasn’t much of a drinker so I ordered some light shots to get things started. He barely got his shot down as he twisted up his face while the liquor burned his chest. I couldn’t help but laugh.

“What?” he said as he gasped.

“You’re funny. You didn’t have to take a shot if you didn’t want. It wouldn’t have offended me,” I said.

“Kate, we came all the way out to this fancy hotel. The last thing I’m going to do is not drink at this bar with all these fancy white folk,” he joked.

I looked around. The bar’s patrons were a mix between happy hour contestants and young players on the prowl. The vibe was casual, but still a bit uppity. The bar tender came to attend our empty glasses as we examined the other patrons.

“Would you like another?” the red headed bartender asked as she wiped the bar clean.

“No. I think we’re fine. We’ll take a beer and a Red Bull. And two waters. Thanks,” I said as I reached for my wallet.

“Stop, I got it,” Rashon said quickly.

“It’s fine. I’m not worried about five dollars,” I snapped.

“Whatever,” he resigned.

“Tough lady! How long have you been together?” the bartender commented. The crows feet behind her red strands of hair made her appear to be around 35. The splotchy tan didn’t help either.

“We aren’t together,” I corrected.

“First date?” she asked us.

We paused before either one could speak. She cut us off. “It’s one of *those* things? Say no more, I understand. One Red Bull, one beer, and two waters.”

I leaned into Rashon as the bartender turned her back to prepare the drinks. “I’m sorry about that. I don’t mind paying. Truth be told I haven’t bought anything fun all year. Let me do me right now.”

He smiled and rubbed my knee. “Kate, Kate, Kate… you’ve come a long way. Remember when you didn’t even want to talk to me? Now you’re offering me free food and drinks.”

The bartender quietly slid our drinks over. She made one of those smiles people make when they don’t want to be rude. Rashon took to his Red Bull and flagged her back over.

“Yeah, can I get some wings? You can put it on the lady’s tab.” he said.

“Rashon!” I hollered.

“Hey, money is not a big deal. You said it yourself. I’m letting you be great right now Kate. *You go girl!*” he hollered back.

“I hate you,” I laughed, “what have you been up to?”

“Chilling’ and working,” he responded.

“You know what I mean. What’s up with you and your new girlfriend?”

“That’s not my girlfriend. Not yet,” he slowly added.

“So you’re saying there’s a chance?”

“We’ve only been out twice. But I talk to her every day. I’m not going to lie. I really like her.”

The wings arrived. I thought of slamming his face into the scorching hot chicken as I eyeballed the steam emitting from the basket. He was being honest, but I wasn’t trying to hear that.

“Are you sure you’re ready for this? How young is this girl?”

"It's whatever. I think every guy wants a woman there for him on some level. You need that cheerleader in your corner. I can't explain it but she does so much for me. A little call or text goes a long day."

"I understand. I'm just so surprised. I thought we were waiting."

"Waiting for what?" he said as he wiped his mouth. His eyebrows arched over the napkin like *The Rock.*

"Waiting to see where this goes. We're close aren't we?"

"Kate, I'm just living my life. I'm not telling you what to do but either way my responsibility is to make myself happy."

"I hear you." I said with a quiet sigh. He was putting the ball back in my court and I didn't want to dribble.

"So what's up with you? How is the international wonder woman doing?"

"I'm working myself crazy, at least I think so," I said.

He laughed and then shook his head. Somewhere in that was a sarcastic comment. I pushed him in the chest playfully as he chuckled. My buzz was beginning to kick in.

"Let's dance!" I said.

"This isn't a dance club," he said as his eyes pursued the bar. There were a couple of blondes on the other side of the bar. They were surrounded by the other men like buzzards. Other than that just about every other guy was single.

"Dance with me," I said as I hopped off the barstool. I grabbed him by the wrists and pulled him into me. My hands traveled his chest and played with his new chain. He smirked as our faces grew closer and closer.

“Kate... Kate…” he said under his breath and shook his head. I turned around to dance back-to-chest and grind my ass on him. He grabbed my hips tighter as he hardened up. The poppy music wasn’t even appropriate to dirty dance too.

BUZZ! BUZZ!

I felt his phone ring. He began to reach for it. I grabbed his free hand and placed it on the side of my breast. The distraction only worked momentarily before he pried himself free.

“I need to go to the restroom. I’ll be right back,” he whispered.

I retired to the bar and ordered another drink. *He must really like that girl.* Some NBA game was on mute on the television. Lebron James dunked on someone, the bar roared over the impressive play. I couldn’t care less about the game but I looked on and waited.

“That type of night?” the bartender asked as she came back around.

“That type of night,” I shamefully smiled.

“It’s none of my business but a guy must be crazy to not want you!” she confessed. I took the compliment without response.

“You got it all going on girl! I’d pay good money to have what you have!” She pretended to have business at the other end of the bar when Rashon showed back up.

“Are you ready?” he asked.

“What’s her name?” I said.

“Kate, you’re tripping. You wanted to go out so that’s what we did. I’m just ready to go home right now.”

“Just tell me her name,” I said. The alcohol was beginning to win. My words slurred a little.

"Mari. Her name is Mari. Are you happy now?"

Without a word I pulled myself from the bar and we headed out of the hotel's front entrance. Rashon was not pleased. He had a prissy attitude as he drove me home.

"Kate, are you the only one here that has permission to have a love life?" he snapped as he steered aggressively in and out of the traffic lanes. I gazed at him for a minute before I held my decision.

"Take me home," I ordered.

He said nothing as he sped and swerved until we got home. The car pulled to a stop in front. This was the part where we were supposed to have an awkward kiss or handshake or something. Only one thing was on my mind. *Finish the mission; put it all on the table.*

"Fuck you," I muttered.

"What's wrong with you Kate?!"

"Fuck you. Come in here and fuck me. Get it over with."

"Kate I think you're drunk."

"You know you want to. You've been waiting to. Come on." I said as I pushed open the door and stammered out. I walked on without looking back. In my drunken mind this was the moment I'd know if he was a serious contender or not. The tension was high. All he had to do was get out, follow me inside and thump me to sleep. If there was ever a time, the time was now.

"Have a good night Kate," I heard him call out. The car then pulled off.

Damn. He must really like that girl.

CHAPTER 7

I debriefed the date with Rashon to Tricia the following day. We came to the conclusion that things were probably best left as they were. I would not push things with him any further. Our platonic relationship was already awkward enough.

Rashon didn't completely stop coming over, but he was becoming conspicuous by his absence. He must have been putting in real effort with the new girl. A part of me despised her and I hadn't even met her. According to what I knew she was some young Caribbean girl who basically treated him like a king. *Whatever.*

Anyways, the second date in the tour was already planned for the following weekend. It was with James who I ran into during the Furniture Depot meeting.

It wasn't hard to get in touch with him. I still had his number in my phone so I just called him up out of the blue. He was pleasantly surprised to hear my voice. Our chat lasted maybe three minutes as we exchanged pleasantries and set up a date. He suggested we'd go to a dog park so I could meet his puppy and then we'd maybe do something afterwards.

Tricia paced across the living room as I explained the situation to her.

"Who is this again?" she asked.

"James. He's the guy I went out with that pissed Justin off," I said.

"I don't remember you telling me about this," she said with a confused look. "How long did this thing last? How far did this go?"

"Just one date, we didn't do anything beyond just hanging out. When Justin found out it triggered the whole turn of events that led to us separating."

"And you think it's a good idea to go out with him again? Isn't it more important to try the Justin thing?"

"We'll get to that. Let's cross the bridge that lies in front," I replied.

"So when is the date?"

"Tomorrow afternoon."

***

I arrived to the dog park approximately twenty minutes early. I watched random pet owners unload their pets and leash them up as I waited in my car. I scrolled through my archived texts while I took my minds off things in a daydream. Rashon hadn't called or texted me in over a week.

Eventually James pulled up in the spot adjacent to me. His dog was no longer a puppy. The terrier looking pup had fuzzy black fur and light brown patches. A big grin was fixed on his face. For some odd reason he shaved off all his black locks and now sported a low crew cut with a thick dark brown beard.

"Me and Nicki getting' married today!" he yelled out of the driver's side window of his black Jeep. I turned down the Nicki Minaj song playing from my car as I laughed at his reference. How he knew so much hip hop culture, I'll never know.

James wore a tight shirt about two sizes too small which showed off his arms and chest which I didn't mind at all. He attached a leash to his pup before we started walking the park's trail.

"Kate this is Hermes, Hermes this is Kate," he said as the dog sniffed my sneakers.

"Hermes? You named him after a clothing designer?"

"No silly! *A clothing designer*," he laughed to himself. "I named him after Hermes the messenger of the Gods. That's Greek mythology. But you wouldn't know anything about that."

"I know the Pantheon looks amazing at night. I love the way the lights hit the sides. You should check it out," I marked.

"You've been to Rome?!" he asked.

"Yeah, for work. The Pantheon and the Coliseum are pretty awesome in person. You'd probably like them especially if you're naming your dog Hermes."

He laughed as he pulled tighter on Hermes' leash. The pup was barking at some of the other dogs in the distance. The afternoon sun felt amazing with the slight breeze out.

"How's life been?" he asked.

"Confusing man, confusing."

"Well, what made you call me after all this time? Do I occupy your mind? Are you confused by *all of this?*"

I broke out in loud hearty laughter. His delivery of the line was perfect, especially since he was walking his terrier that he valued more than life itself.

"I'm confused by a lot lately. I thought I would be happy when I started getting my finances and stuff together, but I'm finding out quickly money doesn't make me truly happy. I'm working so much and making the money so fast I can't even slow down to enjoy it."

"You know what? You sound *exactly* like my brother." he said.

"Oh really? Is that a good thing or a bad thing?" I asked.

"He's always stressed out. I can never get him to relax and do anything. I try to get him to hang out, come to the gym, you know regular stuff. Dude is way too high strung. I'd hate to see you get like that," he said as Hermes sniffed around our toes.

"Too late. I'm already there. You wouldn't believe how many frequent flyer miles I've clocked now."

"I can imagine. How did things work out, you know… with your husband. Again, I'm sorry about that," he began.

"That was over long before you did anything. I already told you that. I'm single as a leaf in the wind," I replied.

"Cool. I don't mean cool like I'm happy, *never mind*," he said nervously.

"Don't worry about it. Anyways, how did the puppies work out?" I asked as we sat at a park bench. Hermes ran around exploring as far as his leash would take him.

"We did well. My ex got a new puppy. A little cute fellow too, he has white fur with the black patches. After we sold all of the other dogs I made a couple thousand. I can't complain."

"Give me the leash," I said as I stood up. I jogged out into the grassy green field as Hermes led the way. James watched as I ran around before returning the dog to him.

"He's so well behaved," I said.

"Want to see something?" he asked. "Heel, up!"

The dog jumped up on its hind legs and walked like a human for a few paces. A childlike beam of pride lit up James' face. He was so amused.

"That's funny. How many tricks does he know?" I said.

"Tons. At least twenty," he replied. The bond between him and Hermes was such a joy to see. He commanded several other tricks to show off for me. I was actually impressed.

"Let's get out of here. What do you have to do for the rest of the day?" I asked.

"Nothing today. I'm off both jobs."

"You're still at BP?"

"Yup, where it all started…"

"You meet any more women at work?"

"None like you," he smiled.

"Well what do you want to do?" I asked as I kneeled down to play with Hermes. The pup had so much energy; we hadn't tired him out a bit.

"I have to buy stuff for dinner. You can join me if you want."

"That depends. What are you making?"

"What do you want?"

"What do you know how to cook?" I countered.

"Kate! Are you coming over for dinner or not?" he commanded. I was pleasantly thrown off by the conviction in his bass-filled voice.

"No," I smirked as I walked off.

"What's up with that?!" he complained.

"You didn't say what you're making," I quipped.

"I can make whatever you want. I can make umm… jerk chicken."

"Why does it have to be chicken? Because I'm black?!" I joked.

"No, no, no… you know what? You're uninvited," he teased.

"Too bad because Hermes already invited me over. So I'm going to join *him* for dinner. You can join *us* if you want."

"That's a deal."

***

"That smells good," I said as I trotted into James' kitchen. He still stayed at the swank, but small, townhouse I visited in the past. He worked over a large stovetop pot. The spaghetti smelled like a heavenly mixture of herbs and spices.

"You like that?" he said. He placed the top back on the pot and stepped back. He leaned in close in an attempt to kiss me. I turned my head slightly. *Too soon.*

The townhouse's first level living room was barely big enough for the single loveseat I retreated to. Hermes ran around my feet as I picked up the coffee table book on the ottoman.

"A designer cakes book? I would have never guessed. I thought you were this big macho guy but you love dogs and bake."

"I don't think that's a problem," James said as he joined me on the loveseat. "I work with my hands all day. Sometimes I like to make something sweet and cuddle something soft. Are you judging me?"

"I'm just surprised," I said as I flipped the book open. Each page displayed detailed photos of big platform cakes and cakes made to look like different characters such as animals. "What else don't I know about you?"

"We only went out one time. How would you know every little thing about me? The unknown is the intrigue. You got to enjoy the slow burn," he commented.

"I mean, I know your brother and we spent enough time together. I just had you pegged for a different type of guy," I shrugged. He snuggled up closer to me and looked over my shoulder.

"I wouldn't mind being on one of those shows like cake boss. That's what I need to be doing. Making big ass cakes and ordering a bunch of flunkies around."

"That sounds like a dream job," I said.

"You're telling me. If I had the money I'd go to culinary school."

"You can't ask your brother to help you out? I'm sure he would. He seems like he cares a lot about you," I said with a soft tone.

"That's the problem. I'm not trying to have my brother take care of me my entire life. Sometimes a man has to step out on his own two feet and make it happen."

"I understand."

"That's encouraging to hear from a woman. My ex was always on me about work. She couldn't understand why I didn't work at Furniture Depot fulltime and why I did my own thing. That was like, one of our major arguments. That and the fact she was crazy."

I chuckled at the joke. I totally understood where he was coming from. He walked his own path. That was a quality I loved to see.

"That spaghetti smells done," I said. He turned off the stove and prepared our dinner. I was feeling a bit too comfortable considering the last time I was here was on the creep. The vibe of this encounter felt like a total 180. James was being the consummate gentleman. I could sense he was checking himself and really trying to win me over.

"I don't have a dining room so either we can eat here or in the room. It's up to you. I don't want to make you do anything you aren't comfortable with," he said, then handed over my plate and fork.

"We're grown. Let's go to your room if it's more comfortable," I said.

"Alright then, lead the way."

By the time we made it to the room all thoughts of food were quickly diminished. Clothes were ripped off at the speed of sound as we got into it hot and heavy, making out and dry humping. My lips engulfed his as we swapped mouth juices.

I could feel myself getting damp. My body was ready for action but my brain still told me to hold back. I could feel his rough calloused hands slide along my sides and underneath my panties. I returned the favor with my own hands as we kissed deeper and deeper.

Eventually I found myself fully topless waiting to be taken to a place of ecstasy. He quickly slipped on a magnum and rubbed around my lips. My legs tensed up as the tension grew. Suddenly my brain interrupted the moment. *Not yet.*

I didn't feel the need to make an excuse. I simply whispered my concerns into his ear. He pulled back at full attention and stopped. I was again surprised how easy going his demeanor was. Everything was almost too good to be true.

I felt comfortable enough so I decided to sleep over the night. James woke me up around the crack of dawn light so I could wash up and prepare to head home. I needed to change for work. It wasn't the exact date I wanted, but I couldn't complain because he was an excellent host. As I drove home the only thing I could think about was the physical encounter.

He was a nice enough guy but there was nothing there. There was no spark. There was no feeling. The only thing I felt around him was the animal instinct to hump like I was in heat. He wasn't the one. At least another stop of the tour was in the books.

CHAPTER 8

“Where did you sleep last night?” Tricia asked as I returned home after work. Rashon was with her, watching some reality show on television. Rashon was totally disinterested in the conversation.

“Stop it, stop it,” I said. “I was just over a friend’s house and crashed there because it got too late to drive all the way back.”

“That’s it?” she said with a smirk that insinuated she didn’t believe me.

“That’s it,” I confirmed.

“You need to get someone to knock you down. Maybe that would loosen up some of that tension,” Tricia said factually. I dismissed her with a quick glance.

“*Anyways.* what have you two been doing?”

“Working and watching *Ratchetball Wives*,” Rashon answered. I laughed at the joke as I took a seat on the couch space next to him. He was steadily texting away as the show played in the background.

“I don’t get why women feel the need to go on these shows,” I said as we watched some girl throw a drink on another. The females got into a full wrestling match on screen. Weaves were pulled, nails were scratched. Any sense of dignity those girls had was gone.

“It’s all about that paper,” Rashon answered. “Women are all about that money. Ya’ll some gold diggers for real. You can’t even find enough men desperate enough to do a show like this.”

“Not all women are willing to go that far for money,” I said as the bleeped out cursing from television played behind me. “I mean… some are, but definitely not all.”

“I know. That’s not how my girl is,” he said matter of fact. My stomach dropped. He was now referring to her as *his girl*.

“How would you know? What’s up with you and that girl anyways? When are we going to meet her?” I said. Tricia leaned back to watch what looked to be a real life scene of *Ratchetball Wives* playing out right in front of her.

“Why do you need to meet her Kate? You don’t have to date her,” Rashon quipped.

“Because I still care about you, dummy,” I responded.

“I’m good. You can stop caring,” he said.

“Shut up! Just let us meet her. One time. If you’re spending all this time with her we’re going to meet her eventually anyway.”

“I’ll think about it.”

“That isn’t the answer I’m looking for,” I said sternly.

“Kate you aren’t my mother.”

“Ok, ok. I’ll back off for now.”

“Why do you feel the need to meet her?” he said after a few seconds.

“Why’ is never a good question,” I said. “You’ll never get the answer you want to hear.”

“I’ll take that as my cue to leave,” he said coldly as he picked himself up off the couch. Something about me was clearly bothering him. I must have pissed him off.

“Don’t be a stranger!” Tricia yelled at him as he left. “It’s been too long.”

“I’ll holler,” he called back as he slammed the door shut.

"What's gotten into him?" I asked Tricia as we continued to relax and watch television. She took a slight breath before answering the question.

"It's all but said and done, he's got a girlfriend. They're serious," she revealed.

"Tricia don't play with me."

"You had your chance girl!" she said excitedly.

"He had his chance as well. Multiple times," I informed. "It's not my fault he didn't want to seal the deal."

She held back a growing laughter as I slumped my head backwards on the couch cushions. Life was beating me down. All of this relationship talk was too much on top of work.

"If I could just combine all of the guys into one I'd have the perfect guy. Let me take this one's money, combine it with this one's humor, and then combine it with this one's aggression," I exhaled.

"How is that tour we talked about going? Are you ready for the last one yet?" she asked.

"I'm not ready to talk to him again yet. I'm still so disappointed about everything," I revealed.

"Kate, regardless of how it plays out, life goes on. You're never going to be ready. Just do it."

"You're right."

***

Aryn pulled me to the side after work to talk again. She seemed to be doing a bit better since the last time we spoke. She had a new smile but that sad aurora still haunted her.

“I made my decision,” she confided to me. I lifted my brow to signal her to continue. I didn’t want to disrupt her speech. It was really difficult for her to talk about these things. She really had to work herself up to approach me each time.

“I told him I was leaving him,” the young girl said as she brushed back a bang of her blonde hair. “I didn’t need to call the police or anything. I just stood up to him and told him I was leaving.”

“How did he take that?”

“He didn’t say anything much. He didn’t do anything,” she shrugged. “He just watched me pack my stuff up and leave.”

“That’s big. I’m so proud of you!” I yelled and hugged her tight.

“I’m worried about him now. He’s been calling and leaving messages threatening to kill himself,” she confessed. “Did I make the right decision?”

“There is a world,” I told her, “A world hidden to only those with the courage to seek it.” She took it every word in as she listened on intently.

“They tell us when we’re young that life is short. That’s not the truth. Life is not easy. Life is hard. Life is long and hard when you don’t make the decisions that lie within your truth. You know deep in your gut what the right decision was and you made it. Don’t let ANYONE tell you otherwise.”

She looked down at the carpeted office floor for a moment to ponder the words I spoke to her.

“Thank you Ms. Kate. I really needed to hear that. I already scheduled a court date for custody but I don’t feel like it’s going to be that bad. Plenty of people have gone through the same thing and lived good lives afterwards. I just feel like no matter what happens everything is going to be okay."

We hugged again. It was a precious moment that I'll always savor. I held on to her like a wise old mother. It felt like I was witnessing my own daughter grow up right before my very eyes. The thin blonde girl was now a strong grown woman in my eyes.

For a moment she said nothing. She simply looked around the office, out the windows, and towards me. Her eyes focused with a new vigor, a new intensity. The gears were turning. She was moving closer to her truth. My work here was done.

***

RASHON

"There is a time and a place for everything," I said calmly like a teacher scolding a child but holding back to spare their feelings.

Mari and I were spending a lot of time together but we still weren't officially exclusive. This date was a gym date that somehow exploded into an argument over Tricia and Kate. She wanted to meet them just as badly as they wanted to meet her. I felt like I was the producer on the set of *Ratchetball Wives.*

Mari spoke between pauses as she laid chest first on the leg curl machine. I looked on to make sure her form was consistent and to check out her ass in the black spandex pants.

"Tell me again how this would accomplish anything," I asked. She counted her set to 10 and paused to rest.

"I want to meet your friends, you have already met my family," she came back quickly. It was partially true. I met her Aunt and her cousin that did her hair, but the rest of her family was still in the islands. Technically she was right.

We switched places so I could do my set of leg curls. I spoke during the rest pauses between each rep.

“You have to watch these American girls. They are all about drama,” I said sternly. There was something shifty behind the need for this meeting on Kate’s side but I just couldn’t pin it down. I could sense however, there was natural competition between the women. They wanted to size each other up but I’d be damned if I ended up dodging drinks like those women on TV.

I finished my set and we exchanged positions again.

“They seem so nice. It will be a great time, just let it happen,” she responded. Her broken accent made everything more exotic and intriguing.

“I’ll think about it but no promises,” I said as she started her reps. “*Time to go! One... two...*”

She finished her set and sat on the bench. “What do you mean ‘NO’?” she exclaimed. “I’ve been doing everything you want from the beginning. You should do some things for me if you want to marry me and live happy ever after.”

My heart skipped and missed a beat. My throat scratched as I swallowed. It was either the workout getting to me or I was getting nervous because of that word. *Marry.*

“Mari, we can meet them if you want. You win,” I said.

She hopped up off the bench and jumped into my arms. I was nearly floored by the big wet kiss she planted on me. I couldn’t lie, I was really falling for the young girl.

“Let’s get out of here,” I said. “That’s enough for one day. You’re already worn out.”

“Yeah, from trying to hang with you! I put my blood, sweat and tears into you. That’s all I got for today,” she said with what little breath she had left.

“That’s too bad. I’m going to really wear you out after this.”

CHAPTER 9

KATE

"I feel like I'm scared of answering the door," I called to Tricia. Two car doors shut outside. They were here. It was finally time for us to meet the new girl.

"Tricia?! Should I open the door? Do I wait for them to knock?!" I nervously stammered.

"Move! Move! I got this," Tricia said as she saved me from the door answering duties. That was my big sis, always fighting the battles I was unable to win on my own. She grabbed me by the shoulder and moved me away from the door. My girl was literally my backbone.

I disappeared to my room to make the transition easier. Seconds later I could hear the clutch of the door open and Tricia greet the new couple.

"I heard so much about you! Come in girl!" Tricia exclaimed. She had that family vibe that could make anyone comfortable. If there was one quality of hers I wish I had, that was it.

"Where's Kate?" Rashon asked.

"She's getting ready," Tricia explained. I took a deep breath before finally emerging from my room. I trotted out to the hallway like a criminal on death row. It was time to walk the proverbial plank.

I turned the corner and there they were. Rashon stood tall in his new casual swag with his girl. I couldn't believe my eyes. She was my spitting image except maybe five years younger. I looked at Rashon, he looked back at me. His eyes said '*please don't do anything.*'

"Hi, I'm Kate," I said as I nervously extended my hand to Rashon's lady friend. Her handshake was flimsy and cold.

"Mari," she replied.

"Nice to meet you," I said with a big disingenuous smile. Rashon looked on with a nervous look similar to that of a man on the Maury show. He had nothing to worry about. I wasn't planning to ruin the evening.

"So where to?!" Tricia asked through the tension filled room. Mari smiled back. She seemed like a sweet girl, though slightly naive.

"What does everyone want?" Rashon asked. We looked on, one after the other, as everyone waited for someone else to speak. Tricia took command as the leader of the group.

"Let's just go to the mall. They have the food court so everyone can get what they want without any problems."

"That makes sense," I replied.

"That works!" Rashon added.

Minutes later we arrived at the mall in separate cars of course. Tricia consulted with me in the car before heading in.

"You good?"

"What do you mean am I good?" I snapped.

"You don't look happy," she said.

"I'm fine. Let's get this over with," I said.

"This was your idea."

"Of course it was," I said as I unlocked the doors. We got out and headed towards the mall entrances. It was a pretty dull day so the foot traffic was minimal. It felt like we had the whole building to ourselves.

"Kate don't say anything crazy. Hold it back," Tricia warned.

"Shut up," I said.

We pushed through the entrance doors and inside to find the rest of our party. Rashon and his girl were walking arm in arm window-shopping in front of a Gucci store. Tricia and I paced behind them slowly, careful not to disturb the couple.

They strolled along as they rambled on about absolutely nothing. I cringed as I overheard the word marriage. The girl was so young she didn't have a clue. Or perhaps he didn't. Island girls were notorious for getting married quickly for legal reasons. I held the thought in the back of my mind as we approached them.

"Are ya'll just going to start shopping without us?" I teased. They turned around to give me a blank stare. Something about the delivery was off. Or maybe they weren't amused. Mari didn't speak much however I could tell she didn't really like me.

"We didn't know where ya'll were at," Rashon said. "Oh yeah! Tricia, we were just saying we should come to your shop one day so you can hook Mari up."

"That's not a problem. I don't know if we have anything to fit you though girl. We tend to carry big sizes. Our main clientele are the big girls, you know, because we got to look good," Tricia said with a confident strut and spin.

"Don't mind her she thinks too highly of herself," I teased to the young girl.

"So what do ya'll want to eat?" Rashon interjected as we changed course for the food court. Tricia and I grabbed some Chinese food while they got pizza slices. We huddled around a square table on separate sides. I sat across from Mari and struggled to make small talk.

Somehow the conversation jumped from the topic of employment to life and relationships. I held back adding any personal details and I noticed Mari did as well. Again some hint about marriage dropped which caused her to finally break her silence. She spoke of it as a certainty. Rashon didn't reject the idea either. They were legitimately infatuated with one another but marriage talk after a few weeks was flat out silly. I couldn't let him make a big mistake.

The evening wasn't that bad. It was a bit awkward but nothing crazy happened. The girl spoke maybe 30 words the entire night. Tricia and Rashon led most of the conversation. From what I gathered Mari was looking for a quick hubby, and Rashon was the easiest target.

After we got home I told Tricia to text Rashon to get him to come over alone. He arrived about 15 minutes after we settled in. Tricia told him some stupid white lie about there being an emergency we needed a man to fix.

"What's going on?! Where is the leak?" he said as he hustled inside.

"We plugged it, sorry. My bad," Tricia said. She quickly disappeared to leave us alone.

"Kate you aren't slick," Rashon offered.

"What?" I replied.

"You guys said there was a leak, where is the water? Where are the mops?" he asked. We were had. "What is this about?"

"Sit down. I want to talk to you," I instructed.

"What are you doing Rashon? Like, seriously?" I asked.

"What do you mean?"

"That girl doesn't know whether she's coming or going, and you're talking about marriage?"

"I didn't say anything about marriage…"

"You didn't say anything against it either," I corrected.

"Kate, I appreciate the concern but it's my life here," he snapped.

"Marriage huh? You sure she isn't hustling you?"

"Here we go," he said as he wiped his brow.

"Rashon I'm from Jamaica. That's how the hustle is worked. You're supposed to find a good American boy and get your papers. I'm not saying she's doing that necessarily but be aware."

"Is that all you wanted to tell me?!" he headed for the door. He was ticked off to the point of almost yelling. With that he reached for the doorknob.

"I just don't want to see you get hurt by anything, especially if I could have said something to prevent it. I'm just looking out for you. I don't feel like you're thinking like yourself right now," I called out.

"I'm sorry you feel that way," he said then shut the door behind him.

***

RING! RING!

I looked over at the illuminated LCD clock. 4:34 AM. Who in the world was this calling me at this time? *This better be an emergency.*

I rolled over and grabbed my cell phone off the nightstand. I didn't recognize the 10 digit number. It looked like an international call. *Who was playing on my phone?*

"Who is this?!" I demanded as I picked up the call.

"Kate, Kate," a strong accented voice called back, "you forgot about me so soon?"

"Who is this?!" I repeated.

"I buy all that furnishing and you don't recognize my voice?"

"Oh. Hi Gio," I said, finally placing the Roman businessman's voice. "Its 4AM in America, is there a problem?"

"I'm just calling to respond to your message," he said. I sent every customer a courtesy follow up email as a way to thank them for their purchase. He wasn't a special case.

"I appreciate it, but it's early here. Do you have any pressing news?" I asked.

"When are you coming back to Italy?" he asked. It was too early for this. I almost ended the conversation there but then I remembered. This was a perfect opportunity to continue *the tour*.

"I have no plans to come back over," I said hesitantly. My eyes started to burn from being stirred awake so long.

"How about you come over for the weekend? You need to see all of what Rome has to offer," he said cunningly.

"Oh really? And are you paying for the tickets?" I asked.

"Of course," he responded bluntly. The offer was dead serious. I just somehow booked myself a weekend excursion back to Italy.

"You have my number. Call me later. American time," I said as the sleep started to get a hold of me again.

"Ok, see you soon."

"Bye."

A few hours later an itinerary and boarding pass showed up in my email inbox. It looked like I was going to Italy. I wasn't expecting to be heading on yet another international flight so soon but this time would be strictly personal and not business. I was actually a little bit excited for it.

The rest of the week at work was mundane and tiresome as usual. I managed my sales team the best I could, continually motivating them to push the phones. I was beginning to feel like I was starring in a real life version of the film *Boiler Room*. We made money but our tactics never changed: dial, dial, and dial.

The weekend finally approached. I was set to hit the nine hour flight on Friday night and return to America on Tuesday. I already had my excuse planned to miss work on Monday. I was going to magically catch the flu and recover within 48 hours.

Since Rashon and I weren't speaking often I grabbed a real taxi to the terminal. I sat in the terminal alone as other families with young children filed in and out. I looked down at my bags. *What was I doing? What was I running to a foreign country for? Was I really this lost?*

DING! DING! "All boarding for flight 4227, Rome, Italy may now proceed!"

There was no time for thoughts. I slipped my iPhone headphones in, grabbed my things for the nine hour flight, and hopped on.

I was already fully awake by the time we landed. The butterflies in my chest were doing back flips by the time I got off the plane. Unlike the previous trips I had a legitimate driver waiting on me when I got outside the airport.

The driver was a nice skinny older gentleman in a slick black luxury car I'd never seen before. He took my bag and then quietly drove me over to Gio's place. It was on the brink of evening by the time I finally arrived.

"How did you like the flight?" he asked.

"It was smooth," I said.

He was still dressed in his work clothes, a half buttoned white shirt with black slack and dress shoes. His hair was slicked back exactly as I remembered. I gave him a routine hug as I trotted inside. The driver brought my bags behind me. Gio quickly tipped him and sent him on his way.

"You look good my lady," he muttered.

"I appreciate it."

"Are you tired?"

"A little, what are you planning for tonight?" I asked.

"A fine dinner and entertainment," he responded. "Are you up for that?"

"I think I can manage," I replied.

The evening was filled with drinks and a world class dinner made by Gio's personal chef who stopped by to prepare the meal. I was blinded by the wining and dining. While I was thoroughly impressed with the meal, the antics of the night weren't over. Before I could even finish my meal a violin player arrived to play us music on cue. It was an intimate breathtaking experience.

"All of this for me?" I said as I washed down my pasta meal with the oaky vintage Gio picked out. He had a very good taste in wine, or the grapes as they say.

"I have something to tell you," he began, and then motioned to the chef to take our dishes. The violin player continued softly in the background. It felt like the slick businessman was setting me up for something. The effort was touching but it still felt too smooth.

I gazed outside. The view of Rome at night was amazing. I could see the whole city lit up underneath us beyond the smallish square windows and open wood shutters.

“What did you want to tell me?” I asked. The mood would have been more romantic if I wasn’t so jetlagged.

“I spoke to my Priest. I told him about you. He told me you would come,” Gio said.

“You asked your Priest about me?”

“You seem surprised. I had a feeling about you.”

“Continue,” I said.

“He told me he sensed a strong desire of the heart and to follow it if the spirit permitted,” Gio responded as he rubbed his gold chain. He wore a crucifix pendant which sat on the middle of his exposed chest. “We should visit the Vatican before you leave.”

“I never knew you were so into faith,” I said, taken back.

“Like anyone I seek understanding. When I am really perplexed then that’s when I seek counsel. You’re one of those cases.”

“I hardly know anything about you,” I casually said.

“What are your intentions Kate? Why *did* you come back? Do you feel anything?”

The violinist finished the final song. Gio tipped him and sent him on his way. The chef finished his duties and left as well. We were finally alone.

“I want to know more about you,” I said. “All I know is that you have a lot of money and you’re a smooth talker. I need to know what's under that. I need to know who Giovanni is. That's why I'm here."

"I worked hard to get where I got. Am I successful? Yes. But there is more to all of this Kate."

"More like what?"

"Do you think I wine and dine every woman I meet?" he asked.

"It's possible. You do own a Lamborghini," I responded sarcastically.

"I'm guilty of living a life of luxury. I don't apologize for reaping my fruit," he began.

"Wait, are you married? Do you have any children?"

"No and no."

"What do you do besides sell your *loan insurance*," I inquired, emphasizing the unethical elements of the business.

"Did I bend a few rules? Is that what you want to know? Sure I did. But I'm not a bad guy. You know that."

"You seem alright," I teased.

"That's absurd! You know I run a legit operation," he said, quickly growing irritated with the personal questioning.

"Calm down. I'm not attacking you!"

"You accusing me of being a liar!" he hollered.

"I didn't accuse you of anything!" I said back.

At this point Gio was full blown upset. He started screaming in incomplete sentences, half in English and half in Italian. I had no idea what he was saying. Maybe my comments ate at a guilty conscience.

"Screaming is not going to get your point across," I warned. His demeanor had completely changed. It felt like I was in a courtroom.

"You are trying to pin those lies on me! I will not sit and allow you to defame my name any further!" he hollered back in broken English.

Since we were in his home and no one knew I was even here I needed to resolve this situation amicably. I did the only thing I knew that could end an argument with an egomaniac man. I agreed with him.

"You're right. You're absolutely right," I began. "I'm sorry. That was disrespectful." The move calmed him long enough to remove him from the conversation. He left me in the dining and living room area as he retired to his room.

I took in the moment. The sight of Italy at night was amazing. It looked nothing like anything back at home. The rigid skinny buildings each lit up from square little windows with antique shutters. There was a certain type of calm in the streets. It wasn't like America with its constant night hustle. Everyone seemed to take a breather at night. I could get used to this.

I later showed up to the bedroom. The place was small so I likely would have to share the bed or sleep in the living room. Gio sat upright in his bed thumbing through a Ferrari brochure. This guy had expensive taste and did not make it a secret.

I noticed a beat up leather bound book on the nightstand.

"What's that?" I asked as the book caught my eye.

"Ferrari. This is the new 430," he said calmly as if the argument never happened.

"No… *that*," I pointed to the book.

"That's my great grandfather's memoirs," he said without lifting an eye away from the vehicle specs.

"Do you mind if I take a look?"

"No. Serve yourself."

The leather bound book held a thin layer of dust that shifted on my fingers as I opened the cover. The pages inside were worn and yellowed, the ink was browning and slightly faded. The manuscript was handwritten by quill, and in old Latin.

I could only make out a few words here and there. There was a long series of short paragraphs written about some sort of love or lover. I could only imagine the old man in his feelings hunched over, quill in hand, transferring every word to the paper.

"See this is the stuff I want to know. There's more to life than fast cars and fast money."

"That's precisely why we are going to the Vatican for Sunday service," he offered.

"Wait… what?"

"Don't worry," he said, "you'll have a good time."

***

The Vatican was the grandest thing I'd seen with my own two eyes. I'd seen it many times before in encyclopedias and on television but nothing was like starting at the real deal. The paintings were so detailed one could see tendons in the muscles of the figures. The energy was calm and almost rejuvenating to the spirit. This was the real deal.

Afterwards we returned to another evening of private entertainment and dining. Gio opened up more about his real life. I learned he was raised by his mother and his father was a vicious businessman. He told me more anecdotes about his upbringing. I learned that Gio was bred to be a cold hearted businessman as well with no plan B. His father pressured him from a young age, it was all he knew.

As far as women went, he was not a stranger to enjoying his fair share of that as well. There were several women who Gio entertained but his paranoia never let him get to the point of seriousness. He made no bones about it that he was open to pursing what lied in our connection but had no plans to settle down. I was not down to be another woman in his harem no matter how much money he had.

CHAPTER 10

“Yes, Italy,” I confessed to my best friend. She had no intentions of my true destination until up to this point.

“Those Europeans love the chocolate. You said he paid for everything?! A chef *and* live music?!” Tricia said in amazement.

“It was romantic I can’t lie. I could see myself living there under the right circumstances,” I replied sprawled out on my homely bed. It was relaxing to finally be back home. I could feel my bones rejuvenate. The nine hour trip had taken its toll on my day.

The weekend was an amazing experience. I wanted it to last forever. Alas, it was over. I was back in the states and back to my regular life. There was little chance I’d ever visit Gio again. There just wasn’t that big of a connection there. Maybe it was the clash in cultures; maybe it was his above the world demeanor. Either way, I was the round peg or he was the square. It just wasn’t going to work out. Another stop on the tour was officially completed.

“What’s up with Shon? Have you spoken to him lately?” I said as Tricia sat on the edge of my bed. She treated me like a child in need of motherly comfort.

“You might not want to hear this, or you may not care,” she began. “He told me he’s going on a trip with her. He plans to ask her to be his girlfriend officially.”

“And where are they going?”

“To some mountain range. I think he said somewhere in Canada. A ski resort type thing.”

“And how can he afford this?” I said springing up in the bed.

“*He can’t*,” Tricia bluntly delivered.

"Lord, Lord. That boy is in too deep," I exhaled and clutched my palm over my forehead.

"You should have warned him how you girls do Yankee boys. Look at what happened to Chris Brown. His career ain't been the same since!" Tricia exclaimed.

"I did. I told him. He wouldn't listen to me."

"What are we going to do about it?" I asked.

"Let him live and learn."

"Tricia I can't do that. He's one of my best friends."

"Maybe you should have let him know that a little bit earlier," she retorted.

"I did. Let's change subjects. You know what I learned so far with this tour?" I began.

"What?"

"I can find things I like in everyone but I can't find everything in one place," I continued.

"That's because you aren't supposed to," she exclaimed.

"Wait, what? Wasn't this whole thing your plan? You mean to tell me there is no point?"

"I didn't say that. I said you aren't supposed to get everything at once. *That's how life works Kate.*"

I exhaled and slumped back in the bed. I felt like a lost newborn child whining to my mother for love and shelter. My heart was pulling in 30 different directions. I had to figure out which way was up. The tour had done nothing other than complicate my love life.

"I know, I know," I replied.

"If you haven't found what you're looking for yet, you know what you have to do. I don't think I need to tell you Kaitlyn."

She was right. I needed to talk to my ex-husband. I had to call Justin. It was time.

***

My knees trembled, my toes itched, and my ears tinged. I took a deep breath and pulled out the folded business card from my drawer.

Knickknacks and More

Justin Rowland (555) 355-4555"

I pulled myself together and dialed the numbers. *Ring! Ring! Ring... click!* Someone picked up the phone. My heart thumped with fear. I brought my mouth to words as quickly as possible.

"Hello?" I said.

"*The number you have dialed has been disconnected. Please check the number and try again.*"

Damn it. I waited too long. The number was no longer in service. I'd just lost the clearest connection to Justin I'd had in over a year. My stomach turned with the thought that I may never see him again. My stomach ached. My breath got thin and thinner. Suddenly, it happened. I. Couldn't. Breathe.

I ran out of my room in a full blown panic attack. Tears streamed down my cheeks. I was unable to let out any audible sound. I flung Tricia's boxes of merchandise as I scoured for help. I fell to my knees. The trauma was unbearable. A sharpening pain drilled in the side of my head. I felt like I was going to die. All I could do was kick the wall as the pain mounted.

Tricia ran to the hallway.

"Kate? Kate! What's wrong with you?!" she hollered.

No response.

"Kate! Kate! Oh my God!" she panicked and called 911. The pain left me curled in the fetal position until the paramedics arrived.

"She's unresponsive! She's not breathing!" I heard Tricia say as my vision blurred and faded to black. I faded and faded into the darkness….

***

Beep! Beep!

The hospital machines hummed in the background as I woke. I tried to speak before I realized I was hooked to an oxygen machine. I snatched the mask off and squinted to focus on my surroundings.

I was propped up in a sleeping gurney with a hospital gown that I did not remember putting on. I looked around the tired, plain hospital room. There was a small television turned on the Oprah channel. A single seat in the corner held a lonely jacket draped over it.

Tricia walked in sipping a cheap vending machine coffee. The corners of her mouth turned up into a smile when she was I was awake.

"Kate, you're awake," she said.

"What happened?" I asked.

"You had a—"

BEEP! BEEP! BEEP! The machine beeped nonstop. A brown skin middle aged nurse scurried into the room. Before I could ask what was happening she forcefully strapped the oxygen mask back on my face.

"Are you feeling better Miss Rowland? I need you to keep the mask on for five minutes. That fresh oxygen should make you feel real good," the nurse commanded.

I shrugged and held my palms up as if to say '*what is going on?'*

"Miss Rowland you had a panic attack. You experienced some shortness of breath and lightheadedness. I need you to keep that mask on," she said. "Do you have a history of such attacks?"

I shook my head no.

"That's ok. There are many different reasons one could have an attack. You could have a trigger such as stress, depression, social anxiety, or any other phobia. You are in good health from what I see."

I closed my eyes and relaxed for five minutes before I could take the mask off. All of the tests proved negative. There was no medical cause of the panic attack but I already knew that. The nurse finished up her files before I saw a doctor for about two minutes. The elderly doctor looked at my files, smiled, and prescribed me to a good night's sleep.

Tricia and I were finally left alone to get out of there and head home. I sat on the edge of the gurney while she sipped her coffee and ate a snack cake.

"I appreciate you calling the ambulance," I said.

"I was so scared girl! You can't do that," she smiled.

"I wasn't trying to scare you. I'm good. It's just that I saw something that made me think about something, then the next thing I knew I couldn't breathe."

"You don't have to explain anything," Tricia said.

"Knock, knock!" a man's voice said as he entered the room. It was Rashon. He was haphazardly dressed in a v neck shirt a size too small and basketball shorts. He leaned in and gave Tricia and I each a hug. I clammily hugged him back.

"I came down soon as I heard," he declared.

"I'm surprised, I really am," I responded. I was happy he cared but I didn't need him to start drama right now.

"Chill out Kate, I come in peace. What did they say happened?"

"Nothing. I just had a panic attack and passed out," I explained.

"I'm sorry to hear that," Rashon answered.

"Where is your girl? Where is Mari?" Tricia asserted. She too was skeptical of Mr. Rashon.

"I told her I had to leave. More important things were happening. I had to get here," Rashon assured.

"I'm fine now, you can leave," I snapped.

"Kate don't be like that. Look, I don't know if you know this but just because I moved on doesn't mean I don't still care about you. I'll never stop caring about you. You and Tricia are like family to me. Ya'll are the only real friends I really have. I love you," he confessed.

"Awww!" Tricia clamored as she mobbed us for a group hug. Rashon held on to me super tight as if he was falling off the Titanic.

“Rashon you can let go now,” I said.

“I don’t want to,” he joked and squeezed harder.

“Rashon stop it! I’m naked under this gown!”

“I know.”

“Get off me! You’re a married man!” I joked.

“Not yet. Not yet,” he said.

“Are you still going on that trip?” Tricia interjected. Rashon looked annoyed she spilled the beans. He finally let me out his grasp and started talking.

“Yeah man, I guess since you already know I may as well tell you both now,” he began. “In a couple days we’re going up to Canada. I plan on making everything official then.”

Tricia conveniently found this as the perfect time to get a refill on her coffee. We were left alone for a brief moment. I stood up and disrobed in front of Rashon. I didn’t care anymore. I smirked as I stood fully nude. His eyes bulged out like a cartoon character.

“I just want you to see what you missed behind door number one,” I mocked.

“I’d show you what you missed but that’s reserved for my girl,” he retorted with his hand gripping his crotch area. “Don’t start something we’ll both regret.”

“Shut up,” I laughed and changed into my regular clothes.

***

The seasonably warm Spring-like day brought out the most vicious bugs known to man on a Sunday afternoon. Tricia and I looked like a modern day Laverne and Shirley in our big Kentucky Derby style hats and matching sunglasses. I dragged her an hour out of her way to come with me to the flea market. Hell or high water, I was going to find my man.

Rashon and Mari had already left for Canada by the time we got on the road. He promised to text us when he got in safely over the border. My heart rooted for him. He deserved to be happy. If Mari was the one who put a smile on his face then I would be less than a friend if I stood in the way of that.

"I'm going to get a headache messing around in this heat," Tricia complained. She was horribly overdressed in some kind of suede leggings with a matching top and over shirt. I was panting with sweat as well in my short set.

We scoured the flea market. It was a vast sea of random faces, families, and vendors about two football fields deep. Green hedges lined the outer boundaries of the market. I looked to Tricia; she was already ready to go. The bugs were getting to her as well and she was hot and pissed.

"Lead the way," she insisted. I looked out through all of the vendors and random patrons. They were all unfamiliar faces. I had no clue where to start. I settled on a far aisle and started walking.

"Let's go over here," I said.

We traveled down the aisle of random antiques and knick knacks. Tricia was definitely out of her element. She was hanging on to support me, which I greatly appreciated. We scanned around looking for out for our target but he was nowhere to be found.

It was a huge market and we had our work set out for ourselves. Tricia thankfully found a vendor with bottled water and bought a couple. I drank the ice cold bottle down in about two gulps. The sun beat down on us harder and harder.

About ten minutes later we'd barely made our way through the first aisle of vendors. This was going to literally take all day because we didn't know where we were going. Tricia was growing increasing annoyed. She started asking vendors the obvious question.

"Do you know a guy named Justin that sells here?" she asked over and over. Each vendor responded negatively, or vaguely remembered someone but couldn't recall exact details.

"Yeah I know Justin!" an older gray gentleman said and pointed towards one of the middle aisles. "He sells over there."

I did my best to hold back a smile. My chest fluttered with anticipation. We scurried over to the both the old man pointed to. I heard someone yell out, "Justin!" This was it.

I pushed my way through the crowded booth his name came from. The exhilaration pent up. I saw the tall figure come into focus with each step. I finally got there. Then I saw him… it was not *my* Justin. I felt like someone played a dirty trick on me. I tried to play the disappointment down as we left the booth.

"Damn it," I said to Tricia.

"Don't get down on yourself. You did the best you could do," she said.

I felt like crying. "What if we don't find him? What if I don't see him again? Tricia, what have I done?!"

She consoled me with a hug. I snapped back into it. We were already here and there was nothing we could do but try to enjoy the day regardless of the objective. We went from booth to booth casually checking out what each person had to sell. Tricia was not impressed with the knockoff versions of some of the same clothes she sold in the boutique. She whispered to me she was making a mental note to snitch at which I chuckled.

RING! RING! RING! Her phone rang.

"Hello?" she answered. It was Rashon.

He told her he and Mari had safely made it in Canada and already at the resort. It felt like he was sneaking to make the call behind his girl's back. I smiled at the notion of him sneaking off to make an inconsequential call. He promised to call or text back when he dropped the news on her. Tricia wished him good luck and hung up.

I was dead. The sun successfully beat me down. I scrambled for an open wood bench I spotted out the corner of my eye. I needed to sit down and try to recover from the sun as best I could. Tricia walked over at her own pace and joined me.

"What do you think?" she said.

"What do I think about what?" I asked.

"Rashon and his girl, do you think she will say yes?" Tricia added.

"Of course. Would she talk about marrying him with no intentions of being exclusive?"

"Crazier things have happened," she went on.

"True."

"Are you ready to go?" she asked.

"I guess so." I was defeated. It was a lost cause. The day was officially wasted. This stop in the tour was obviously too late. I resigned to the defeat. *Maybe I'll catch him on Facebook.*

"Before we go let me check out this girl over there in the corner. She looks like she has some fake Balenciaga bags. I need to make sure I get her too."

"You're a snitch!" I laughed.

"Girl, they lucky I don't cut them *and* the bags up right now. They're taking food off my table. I don't play that!"

I chuckled more as she led the way over to this girl's booth. The girl was a hustling middle aged Puerto Rican lady simply trying to make some extra cash. Tricia pretended to be interested in purchasing the bags as she inspected them up-close for flaws and obvious signs of counterfeit.

"This one is good," she mused and showed to me.

The bag looked exactly like one of the ones I'd seen in the house. Minus a few minor flaws here and there one could not tell it wasn't the real deal. Only a trained eye like Tricia's could spot out the missing details.

Tricia took the seller's card and stuffed it in her pocket with cards of about three other sellers she planned to snitch on. I decided to take one last crack at my mission before we left. I called for the woman's attention.

"Excuse me! Do you know a guy that sells here named Justin? He's a white guy about 6'2, brown haired with blue eyes," I questioned.

She held a puzzled look for a few moments and squinted as if she was trying to recall something. Her index finger tapped her bottom lip as she thought on it. Finally she held an answer.

"The name sounds familiar. But I don't think he matches the description you gave," she apologized.

“It’s okay. Maybe I have the wrong flea market or something,” I commented. I finally caught up with Tricia who was steering her way around the flea market with her own mission in mind.

“Let’s get out of here before you get everyone in here caught up,” I smirked.

CHAPTER 11

"Before we get out of here I have to take you to one of my favorite spots," I said as I steered around.

Justin and Tricia lived about an hour or so apart but I'd hung out down here many of times. I had to take Tricia to one of my favorite restaurants in the area as a 'thank you' for wasting her day with me. I headed for *Bob's Cook Out*, my favorite family burger spot that was more famous for its shakes than actual food.

I pulled into the lot and parked right in front of the small dingy brick building. I instructed Tricia to get out and follow me inside.

"They have the BEST milkshakes here. Get whatever you want, my treat," I insisted.

The old African American family that owned the place greeted me with the usual warm welcome I'd come to expect. Tricia perused the menu to see what she wanted. I already knew what I was going to get, the Oreo cookie shake with vanilla ice cream. My buddy finally settled on a peppermint shake with chocolate chips.

We took a booth seat to chill out. It was a long time since we'd just chilled as girls. It felt like old times again.

"What do you think about that?" I asked as she devoured the sweet milkshake.

"It's good. You have good taste," she replied.

We quietly enjoyed our treats and each other's company. The conversation drifted through the regular topics of work, life, love, and entertainment. Tricia's boutique was doing really well. I was chugging along on my path yet unfulfilled.

Other customers came in and out. The spot was getting a little busy with the flea market winding down. It seemed like everyone had the same idea. In a span of about ten minutes at least thirty people made their way in and out the little diner.

DING! DING! Tricia's phone went off. She showed me the new text from Rashon. Mari and him were official. She texted back our best wishes and left him to enjoy his trip. That got us back on the topic of life and relationships.

Tricia's love life was a complete mystery to me. Sometimes there would be contenders but no one ever actually won her over. Tricia was a lot to handle for one guy, literally and figuratively. You had to come 100% correct if you wanted to step to the curvaceous fashionista.

"Girl I don't have time for these wannabe's. I need a *real* man to step up and take charge. I need someone who can handle me and tell me what to do," she loathed.

"You like those roughnecks," I began. Her jaw dropped as if I just shattered her reality. She squinted like she was seeing the sun after a lifetime in the darkness. She had a problem dealing with whatever she was thinking.

"Are you alright?" I uttered as I slurped the bottom of my milkshake.

"….there's…. there's your husband behind you," Tricia stammered.

"You're not funny. Don't play with me," I remarked as I turned around. My stomach dropped. Tears burned in the corner of my eyes, my nose burned. All of the thoughts in my mind evaporated at once. It was him. It was Justin.

He had on a gray thermal top and beat up jeans. It looked like he'd been outdoors working all day but it didn't matter. He was *here*. I stared into the bold blue eyes I couldn't get out of my mind as he took the seat next to me in the booth.

"Wow… Kate. What are you doing down here?"

"We came to the flea market. We came to see you," I barely managed to get out.

"I wasn't even going to come here but I woke up with a craving for a milkshake," he said. Just being in his aurora felt right. There was so much I wanted to say at once. I couldn't let him go again. Tricia felt the energy change and quickly made herself disappear. Justin and I were left alone.

"What did you think about the market?" he asked with his vanilla shake.

"It was crazy busy. Were you even there? I tried to call you," I revealed.

"I lost my phone," he shrugged. We laughed together. It was just like old times. Justin was never a phone person. He'd rather die than have to deal with the nonstop phone calls and text messages.

"How are you doing? I worry about you," I asked.

"I try but it's not easy. God or whoever isn't done with me yet though," he declared. "What have you been up to Ms. Professional?"

"Work is killing me but I'm doing well. I really like what I do."

"That's good to hear. Kate, again, I'm sorry about the way everything worked out. I shouldn't have hid my lifestyle from you. I was so afraid of bringing you down with the drugs and everything."

I nodded silently as the tears broke and streamed down. He was broken but Justin was still in there. He was a lot livelier than the last time I'd seen him. It was in that moment I knew that we made a mistake.

"Oh yeah, I quit the Zoloft. See, I listen to you," he chuckled. "I still can't kick the marijuana though. The depression is still too much."

"What happened to therapy? You can't go back? This isn't your fault. You're sick," I begged.

"I'd quit if I could but it's all I got. I can't afford to continue therapy. Long story short my insurance dropped me."

"Justin I can pay for it. I can afford it," I commanded.

"I can't accept that," he replied. He looked distantly off in the wide diner windows.

"I want to. I still love you."

"I messed everything up. I lost everything. I can't let you buy my love. I'm not good for anyone right now," he shook his head.

"You never lost me. If there is one thing the last year taught me is that no man can replace what you give me. No one makes me laugh like you; no one appreciates me like you do. I'll pay for the rehab and I'll be here for you when it's over."

"Kaitlyn… I can't let you do that," he insisted.

"I'm not giving you a choice. You're going to rehab. It's not even about us anymore. You're funny, smart, and intelligent; you have a lot to offer the world. I can't let you throw that away!"

"What about us? Where do we go from here?"

"We can start over," I said.

Our fingers locked. I leaned and wrapped my arm around him. Our faces inched closer. Finally our lips touched. I drifted off into heaven. It was right. This is where I was supposed to be.

FIN

MESSAGE FROM THE AUTHOR

Thank you for purchasing *The Ex's Tour.*

This novel is the third and final installment in the *Dishonorably Discharged* series; however some characters may be in a new series going forward. As the series grows and focuses on the other characters it only makes sense for the title to move away from an event which happened in the first book. With that said please be on the lookout for my new stories!

As a small publisher it is difficult to gain traction and I appreciate everyone who purchases, reads, and downloads my work. If there is any spare time you have after reading I ask that you **please leave a review** at the book retailer! This REALLY helps me out.

Again, I thank you for your purchase and appreciate it greatly. As a token of my appreciation there is a bonus preview of my novel *Wrestling the Russian* included.

Thanks!

Stay in the loop on future releases, updates, and special offers.

Join the exclusive email list today:

Click Here to Join

SPECIAL PREVIEW:

Wrestling the Russian

Available now!

***

The ride home was terribly silent. Yegor was mulling in depression and Chad was too afraid to speak. I had to do something to break the ice. I confronted the issue head on. It was all I knew.

“Do you know why they only picked you Chad?” I asked. Chad’s eyes fearfully cut at me in the front seat. He didn’t want to discuss this in front of Yegor.

“Who knows? Wrestling is a unique business,” Chad quickly said.

“I’m asking because both of you did well, you two had the best match in my opinion. There has to be a reason they only want you,” I said.

Chad was not cool with the conversation. He quickly changed topics.

“Mark says he can give you two rides while I’m in Orlando. I’ll be right back. It’s nothing serious. It’s not like I’m going straight to the main stage.”

“You’re not coming back,” Yegor spoke up from the back seat. The tension could be cut with a knife. “That’s not how it works. Once you’re in Orlando you’re in WWW. You’re not coming back.”

“But I don’t get it. Why would they only take one of you?” I asked.

“That’s not your problem,” Yegor said. The car stopped. We were at Yegor’s place.

It was probably the last time he’d see Chad for a while. Yegor didn’t care. He slung his gym bag over his shoulder and got out. He issued his usual cold thank you and entered his apartment building.

Chad pulled the car into reverse as we began to leave. Something in my stomach shifted. This wasn’t right. I had to do something.

"Stop!" I said to Chad. He looked at me like I was crazy. I got out the car.

"Brianna what are you doing?" Chad called to me. I ignored him as I sprinted back to the building.

I was out of breath by the time I got to the door. I quickly flung it open and ran down the hallway, each step burning my chest as I was completely out of breath. I got to the end of the hall. There was another hall. I scanned left, then right. That's when I saw him.

"Yegor!" I forced out of my drained lungs. He stopped in place, looking at me with puzzled eyes.

"What do you want? Why are you here?" he asked as I ran over to him.

"This has to stop. You cannot do this forever. Why do you act like this?" I asked. He turned his head, avoiding eye contact once again.

"Why do you care?" he said.

"Because I do! People care about you. We want to help you and you just push us away!" I yelled back.

"I'm not talking about this here. Come inside," he commanded.

I walked shoulder to shoulder with him to his apartment a few doors down the hall. He unlocked the door and led me inside.

Yegor's place was very modest. It was a studio apartment with nothing more than a bed, computer, and a table. Scattered across the studio were half empty bottles of protein powder and Gatorade. There were also books. A lot of books.

He slung his gym bag on the bed. "Say what you have to say," he instructed.

"See, why do you have to be like this?" I asked. I sat down on the bed as he mulled around.

"Why do you care about me?" he asked again. The fact that I already answered the question once obviously was not good enough for him.

"Because I like you, you idiot!" I yelled at him. He was stunned. He said nothing; he just looked at me with a look I'd never seen before behind his thick black beard.

"You play like you're this tough guy, but your actions say otherwise. You've helped me with everything since day one. You even told Mark to let Chad work as the face because of what happened to him in the past. You wanted him to get invited to Orlando. *I know,*" I replied as he said nothing and me down.

"Really? You're still going to play tough guy? There's no one here but you and I," I said.

"You don't know anything about me. I'm not a good guy," he sighed then broke his silence. He was committed to the act. I was determined to break him down.

"Tell me about you then. What happened so bad that you can't drop the attitude for just me?" I said. He walked slowly towards me as his demeanor softened a bit.

"I am an orphan, and an immigrant. I was sent here when I was two years old. I've never met my parents. I don't know what happened to them. I've never been told what happened or why I was sent here. I'm just here."

"I grew up in Oakland, California. I was a poor immigrant with no money. No parents. The people who raised me weren't even family; they were just people who were told by whoever in Russia to take care of me. No one has ever explained anything to me. Wrestling is the only thing I can do to make a decent living, well, if I was in

WWW and you already know that story," he continued as I took it in.

"But you're a good guy. Why act this way? I know you care about others. You can't even pretend that you don't," I cut him off.

"That doesn't mean anything. You need to realize that. It's not about words. Your country is backwards. You'd rather say you care and not insure accountability. Most don't give a damn. That is fact," he responded.

He sat down on the bed his hand grazed my leg. It slowly crept up closer and closer. I grew anxious. I took a deep breath as he looked me in the eye.

"Brianna, you have a lot to learn. You're a very pretty girl. You weren't bad before you got in shape either. You'll go far in this business. We have to train tomorrow and you have a ride to catch."

He got up and walked with me to the front door of the building. Chad was still outside waiting in the Impala.

"Goodnight Brianna," Yegor said as I got back in the car.

Chad was astonished. He asked me what was going on as we drove off. "What did you say to him?"

"I just wanted to make sure he was ok," I replied as Chad nodded.

"Oh, and what happened?"

"I learned a little more about why he is the way his is," I said.

"And why is that?" Chad asked.

"He's a crazy Russian guy."

----

http://www.DeseanRambo.com

Also by Desean Rambo:

All's Fair in Love and Football Series

Dishonorably Discharged: A Love Story

Wrestling the Russian

Available at eBook retailers near you!

http://www.DeseanRambo.com

deseanrambo@boardgamemedia.com

www.ingramcontent.com/pod-product-compliance
Lightning Source LLC
LaVergne TN
LVHW012114160826
845678LV00014B/3094

* 9 7 9 8 3 7 3 9 0 0 2 6 3 *